The Other Side of the Universe

The Other Side
of the Universe

Kurt Dreifuss

TWAYNE PUBLISHERS
New York

Copyright, © 1961, by Kurt Dreifuss

Library of Congress Catalog Card Number: 61-9275

MANUFACTURED IN THE UNITED STATES OF AMERICA BY
UNITED PRINTING SERVICES, INC.
NEW HAVEN, CONN.

TO MY WIFE

*For her patience and loyalty
during the many long hours
she has had to spend alone
while I was away on voyages
to the Land of the Vinibins*

FOREWORD

The events related in these pages happened quite a long time ago—long, that is to say, before the still explosive scientific discoveries of the last ten years brought into being an entirely new historical age, the age of atomic power and space flight.

In one sense, they seem to have happened a very long time ago, yet in another, only yesterday. The contradiction stems from the fact that a year today is like a hundred or even a thousand years in the past, if one measures time in terms of man's material progress. For example, it seems only yesterday that people regarded as mere foolishness such talk as sending a man-made satellite about the Moon, or building a space station in the Earth's outer atmosphere for a jumping-off place to other planets, or training pilots for space trips to the far corners of the Universe—foolishness, suitable for juvenile fiction or for dreamers contemplating the never-to-be millennium. Yet, overnight it has become eminently practical to discuss such things, while a half dozen nations are racing to be the first to make the trip to Mars or the Moon!

So, in one sense, the incidents about to be described occurred very recently; to be more precise, early in June of 1926. Reading more like fiction than fact, they followed in the wake of a series of aeronautical tests conducted by Timothy Jones, a then obscure young engineer employed by the now defunct Abbott-Swift Laboratories of Chicago. The company did metallurgical research in the early days of the aviation industry.

Jones' findings held some startling revelations which went far beyond their immediate bearing on his assignment. But, as sometimes happens, they were unlooked for and thus unrecognized at the time, and there were just enough missing parts in the picture to conceal their significance. It must be said to Jones' credit, as the record will show, that he had at least a fleeting awareness of what he had actually stumbled on. But even if he had seen clearly beyond the missing parts and caught the full meaning of his partial evidence, it is highly improbable that he could have gained a serious ear from academic people or the public generally. As a young man of limited scientific background working in a secondary technical capacity for a commercial engineering concern, he had hardly the kind of professional standing that would have permitted him to advance with authority theories of "Einsteinian" proportions. Furthermore, his findings, if expounded with any degree of vigor, no matter by whom, would have been so badly out of tune with the whole Time Spirit of the 1920's as to have sounded as absurd as some of the fiction thrillers of the day about space men invading the Earth with bombs capable of destroying us all!

*　*　*　*

With these brief introductory remarks to serve as a point of reference, the author is eager to present this unusual account. It might perhaps best start with events immediately following Jones' last test flight and a near crash landing which, while leaving the plane intact and the pilot uninjured, ended forever any further experimentation.

The Other Side of the Universe

I

Timothy turned the nose of the plane from the sea. He hadn't the faintest notion where he was. Certainly, he had no idea he had landed on the shores of Vinibus! Dazed and exhausted from a bewildering air experience, he could only breathe a sigh of relief at the sight of land.

In the distance below he could see the yellow sands of a beach. Through a cloudless yet murky sky he could discern low hills extending from the shore, some thickly wooded, others covered with vineyards and fields. As he lowered the craft, clear water streams came into view winding their way, like thin threads of mercury, through rich, green fields in the valleys.

The plane made a perfect landing, then taxied over the smooth sand of the beach. The lone pilot jumped out, glad for the feel of solid earth under his feet. He looked eagerly about. From the shore which stretched in an irregular line along the ocean, the land could be seen to slope gradually to the water's edge to afford a view of the country for many miles inland. But the scene immediately to the rear of the beach was obstructed by low trees heavy-laden with tropical foliage. The branches drooped in long, green strands almost to the ground. Timothy stepped toward the trees to reconnoitre, but as he did so his knees buckled and he had a sudden feeling of utter exhaustion. Young and adventuresome though he was, this flight had been more than he had bargained for. The whole thing was yet as inexplicable to him as it was presently to be revealing. He made his way back to the plane, and as he started to enter the cabin

11

there was a rustling in the trees along the beach. Something was forcing its way through.

What he saw put his already jaded nerves on edge. There emerged from the bushes a strange looking beast which made directly for him. The creature kept coming closer, and the young man continued to stare at it, too terrified to move. It was about the size of a deer, with the striped body of a tiger, and a long, giraffe-like neck, and thin, hair-covered legs. At the upper end of the tall neck protruded an ungainly, uninviting looking head.

Timothy made a dash for the cabin. As he took hold of the door, he heard a woman calling to the animal in a soft musical voice. He looked and saw the beast stop short in its track, while the woman, attired in a flowing garment and speaking a foreign language, appeared to be scolding it. The animal stood for a moment as if unable to decide whether or not to obey its mistress, then, seeing the stranger apparently for the first time, effected a most comical turnabout and scampered with all speed toward the woman.

The woman held the unsightly creature close at her side, and, as she looked up, brought one hand to her breast in a gesture of fright while the other remained protectingly about the beast, which buried its head ostrich fashion in the folds of her dress.

Puzzled and amused, Timothy came within speaking distance, but the woman, visibly agitated, retreated back toward the trees. He tried a friendly greeting but she made no answer. She seemed ready to disappear behind the trees should he come any closer.

He ventured an apology for his intrusion.

"Sorry, Miss—I had to make a forced landing." He pointed to the plane.

Still no reply. Only that glance of wonder. He made another effort.

12

"Can you tell me where I am? This place," he indicated with a sweep of his hand, "looks unfamiliar." He tried to ingratiate himself with a smile. But again no answer; again that bewildered stare.

"You do not understand?"

Quite obviously, she did not.

As her eyes wandered again irresistibly from Timothy to the plane, he had an opportunity to approach closer.

It was now his turn to feel surprise. The woman was young and beautiful—strikingly beautiful. While at a distance, and engrossed in his own problem, he had not observed her features. Now he gazed with rapture upon the exquisite lines of her face and body. He felt as one entranced, oblivious to everything but the charm of her presence.

She was tall and slender, with an unusual grace of bearing. Her face held a warm, feminine loveliness, and her skin, delicate and smooth, was yet vibrant with youth and health. Her eyes were large and soft, and they seemed to penetrate the love-stricken youth's whole being with a tender magnetism. Her hair, tucked lightly at the back, was neither blond nor dark, but it had the lustre of spun gold as it shimmered in the sunlight.

Timothy stared with unconcealed fascination. The flowing gown which had appeared theatrical at first now became transformed to a thing of surpassing beauty by the loveliness of the person wearing it. It was made of a soft brown material, lavishly but artistically figured in gold and black, and it flowed loosely from her shoulders. Of simple, classic design, it was skillfully fashioned to set off the beauty of bodily form.

But her face! Timothy was strangely moved by it. Not an intellectual face nor a frankly robust one, it seemed to hold a subtle combination of all the attributes of feminine allurement. To Timothy it was the kind of face that all men vaguely visualize when they dream of their ideal woman, their Goddess!

The woman, quick to discern his feelings, smiled now and permitted him to come closer. She spoke a few words that sounded foreign to his ears. She beckoned for him to follow.

They passed through the narrow opening in the trees, she leading the way, followed closely by the now gentle looking beast and Timothy. As they emerged from the bushy trees, vistas of strange vegetation opened on either side of them, some tropical, others characteristic of the temperate zone. The profuse, unorthodox assortment of plant life served only to heighten a very much confused young man's curiosity.

Soon they came to a cluster of trees and shrubbery. Through the foliage Timothy could see an odd looking structure projecting considerably above the surrounding trees, and blending in color and form with the vegetation. To the casual observer, at even a short distance, it was quite invisible. Timothy's guide turned to him and nodded. This was evidently her home.

It was a queer place, its architecture unfamiliar, its plan of construction unlike anything Timothy had ever seen. He regarded it with confused feelings, confused thoughts crowding his brain. He really couldn't decide whether it was ugly or fantastically beautiful. It made him think of the words of a famous nature lover: "The totally strange or hitherto unheard-of can never appear beautiful, because that which is most unreal in it attracts too much attention and is given undue prominence in the picture; and we miss that which would have taken away the effect of strangeness—the perfect balance of the parts and the harmony of the whole."

The entire structure rose massively from the ground, taking on an aspect of nature's delicate foliage as it towered

14

upward. The coloration was profuse, with hues of green, yellow and gold, of brown and red, all ingeniously blended after the pattern of pigmentation in plant life. The lower portions were pale green, and seemed to take natural root in the ground, while the higher parts, rising in oddly shaped turrets to great heights, changed gradually into deeper and richer shades, until, at the top, they became a burst of reds and yellows and blues as of myriads of flowers. In its bizarre appearance, the place combined something of the primitiveness of a grass hut with the architectural finesse of the most modernistic of dwelling places. Withal, it looked like some freak colossus of nature towering majestically over its earth-born neighbors. The trees and flowers that surrounded it on all sides looked like obedient vassals swaying and nodding in silent homage.

Timothy gazed in wonder. His companion observed him quizzically, then beckoned again for him to follow. He needed no urging. When they came to the entrance of the house she turned to him to indicate that they had arrived at their destination.

They were met at the door by a middle-aged man, robust looking and short of stature. He was clad in dark knee-breeches and an orange colored shirt made of fine silk. The shirt was open at the neck and had sleeves just long enough to cover the shoulders. Ankle stockings and sandals adorned his feet, and his exposed legs and thighs were muscular and solidly built. His skin was thoroughly bronzed by the sun, and he might easily have been taken for an Alpine or a Scotch Highlander but for the unfamiliar style of his bright colored garb.

The man greeted them cheerily, but his face showed great surprise at the sight of Timothy. He looked at the woman for an explanation, and she in turn regarded Timothy with an expression that seemed almost to denote pity.

Evidently her guest though young and not bad looking had aroused none of the ardor in her that she had in him. She made a remark to the man, whereupon he opened his eyes in astonishment and rushed down to greet Timothy with great solicitation. With a sweeping bow he invited him into the house.

Timothy's two hosts now seemed to vie with each other in their gestures of welcome. He was offered a rustic chair made of the timber of young trees, for which he was indeed grateful because he felt his fatigue returning. The chair, despite its rough appearance, was comfortable, and Timothy gave a sigh of relief. The man now began eagerly to ply him with questions; but his language was as unintelligible as was that of the woman. They tried to make themselves understood by signs and motions, and at last succeeded in conveying their names to him. The man was called "Bornabi," and the woman, "Vergia." From their behavior he took them to be father and daughter.

When Timothy's turn came to introduce himself, there was great difficulty. His first name they simply could not pronounce. The word "Jones" was baffling too but they could make something of it. The "J" they pronounced like a "Y." The "S" they could not utter at all, and the "E" got undue emphasis; so that the name became "Yonné."

And Yonné it was to be! Efforts at introduction got no further on either side. So far as Yonne, erstwhile Timothy Jones, was concerned, there was indeed, not much more that could have been said about him at this time, had they understood each other perfectly. He was twenty-seven years old with no outstanding achievements and no unusual habits. A product of World War I, he had drifted along with the uncertainty of the times, without ambition or urge to take stock of himself. The world of business had held no lure for him, and he had just entered his junior year at Armour

16

Tech when the war broke out. Pilots were needed, and he met the emergency requirements with a sound body, a sound mind, and the adventuresome spirit of youth. Afterwards, he went into the hazardous occupation of test flying because flying was the one thing he knew, and knew well. Evenings he finished his college studies at Armour, then got the job at Abbott-Swift.

In a real sense, Yonne was yet as much a stranger unto himself as he was to his strange hosts. There were latent qualities in him, but of these he was only dimly aware, and they were buried deep under a stereotyped, technical education. Had it not been for the present aeronautical mishap, he might never—but this is getting ahead of the story.

As he looked about the home of his hosts, Yonne became obsessed with an unaccountable feeling of faint familiarity, as though he had seen all this some long time ago but couldn't quite place it—a sense of closeness which kept forever eluding him, like a kind of amnesia that seems about to lift its hold upon the memory.

Suddenly, he had a feeling of apprehension. He got up and walked nervously about, his eyes searching eagerly some clarifying object. But there was nothing. He could see only that everything about the place was a domestic replica of the world of nature without, and that there was something ancient about it—something that reminded him of the pagan days of ancient Greece or Rome.

Antiquity—that was it, thought Yonne, a vague, uneasy sense of ancient timelessness possessing him and setting up in his mind a train of weird associations.

He looked about and saw that the elegant interior had the characteristic, ornate courts and fountains, the colonnaded chambers, of Roman times. The rooms were flanked, however, not by the classical type of column, but by immense pillars imitative of trees which rose massively to some forty

17

feet, spreading their foliage to serve as framing for the ceiling and giving an irregular, domelike shape to the rooms. They lent a restful, sylvan atmosphere to the place.

Yonne saw that furnishing and household pieces were all patterned after some form or artistic version of the plant or animal world. Machine production seemed to have had little part in their manufacture. Everything was wrought by the hand of some skilled artisan. In a pleasing way, the entire effect was one of outdoor ruggedness combined with a warmth of domesticity. Certainly, nothing about the place was "modern" in our sense of the word, the very atmosphere breathing an air of antiquity.

Yonne looked at the woman, and he was thrilled anew at her exquisite beauty. She seemed like some ravishing princess of ancient Nineveh or Babylon, her lovely form given a touch of unreality in this unworldly setting.

Unworldly?

The thought struck him. At a far corner of the room he spied a terrestrial globe mounted on a pedestal, and he rushed over to examine it. With nervous impatience he rotated it, his fingers running quickly over the surface markings. The usual configurations of land and water were not there. Continental formations were unfamiliar.

He felt little beads of perspiration coming out all over his body. He dared not believe what he saw.

Again he scanned the globe's markings. Everything was different: strange configurations; strange topography; strange oceans and continents. Across his mind flashed a premonition of what had happened: He was no longer upon Earth!

Preposterous!

He clutched the globe and glanced at Bornabi and Vergia. They observed him intently and exchanged knowing glances.

They knew!

It was incredible. He tried to compose himself. He paced

18

the floor seeking to piece together the events that had befallen him, but they made no sense. His seemingly time-less, inexplicable adventure in the air was a total mystery. But this—this thing could not have happened.

With maddening persistence, the thought became fixed in his mind: He had transcended interplanetary space!

His scientifically trained mind revolted against the idea. The element of time, of distance, of temperature—these and a host of other things all pointed to its sheer im-possibility.

He looked at Bornabi and Vergia. They were standing at his side, silent and bewildered. He walked to another part of the room, and came face to face with the most tell-ing bit of evidence—himself. There in the mirror before him was reflected his image. His clothes were dishevelled, his collar and shirt open, his hair was in disorder.

On his usually smooth shaven face was a three weeks' growth of beard! His hands went trembling to his face to feel at his sunken, unshaven cheeks.

"Is it possible?" he gasped.

Bornabi and Vergia seemed to nod their heads.

II

Things now happened quickly and with devastating certainty. It had grown late in the day. The sun had gone down and the twilight had lent a soothing atmosphere to the place. A cool breeze stirred, and Yonne felt an irresist-ible drowsiness come over him. Bornabi observed him sharp-ly and spoke quickly to his daughter.

The rest transpired as through a veil of semiconsciousness. His hosts, half carrying and half leading him, took him up to one of the turrets. They gently loosed his clothing and helped him to a small cot where he fell at once into a heavy sleep. Soon he was tossed about by restless dreams. Bits of his aeronautical adventure, crazy and distorted, flashed before his eyes:

He was flying again through the upper stratosphere at the very fringe of the Earth's gravitational pull. He had brought the plane into orbit as planned. It raced along its prescribed arc about the Earth. All went well.

Then something happened. The craft suddenly veered from its orbit and headed straight for outer space. Desperately, he sought to bring it back under control and on its course, but to no avail.

It was a matter of seconds. The plane's instruments failed to respond. The oxygen and pressure equipment ceased to function, and the air in the cabin grew thin. Yonne felt faint, he gasped for breath, then blacked out.

He seemed to regain consciousness but he was no longer in the plane. He was poised alone in space. He felt giddy, as though mind and body were detached. All the heavenly bodies were dancing before his eyes. Fiery planets whirled about in every direction, shooting stars and comets and spiral nebulae.

At times things grew quiet and dark again; then, the Earth appeared on the horizon, large and round and yellow as the moon. Slowly it sailed across the sky as upon a vast sea and it cast a pale light over all the heavens. Once it became suddenly transformed into a face, hazy and indistinct. He tried to make it out, but it was enshrouded in a mist. Then the mist cleared and he saw the face was Vergia's. Before her loveliness all else faded. Gazing down upon him, gently, lovingly, she descended close to his bed, her tender eyes speaking of love, her sensuous lips almost upon his. She beckoned him on. He tried to draw her close, but she vanished in his grasp.

Now he was in the plane again flying at incredible speed. The artificial little space capsule with its human occupant flicked through cosmic space like a tiny fragment of dust, without seeming direction.

On and on it raced . . . 20 . . . 30 . . . 40 miles per second . . . the speed of heavenly bodies. Yonne calculated wildly: Soon he would arrive at the Earth's nearest planet, 30 million miles away. That was his goal!

Alas, it seemed impossible . . . 30 million miles! But it had to be done. Ah, but the distance was interminable . . . an eternity!

Fatigue was upon him again, then sleep . . . deep, heavy sleep. His head dropped forward. His arms fell limp to his side. The new world could not be reached . . . the goal was lost!

Before his closed eyes, the old Earth came again into view, a sardonic grin playing upon its face. Then slowly it receded into the dark background. In his ears rang a harsh, mocking laughter.

His dream seemed to come to a sudden end as the whole Universe exploded in a splurge of light.

* * * * *

Yonne sat up in bed with a start. It was morning. Seated at the bedside, observing him closely, were Bornabi, Vergia and a newcomer dressed in gay peasant garb. All three had been laughing pleasantly about something. Now the men turned to each other—Bornabi with a sigh of relief, the stranger with a broad grin. The stranger felt his pulse, and, patting him on the shoulder, gave some hurried instructions to Vergia, rose and bowed a gracious exit. Vergia followed

21

him but returned at once with a tray of food consisting of boiled cereal, rough bread, honey, butter and a delicious beverage. He rubbed his head trying hard to remember what had happened. Despite his nightmare, he had a feeling of exhilaration. Also, he was ravenously hungry and ate everything they put before him.

It was embarrassing to be fed in bed while his mind was groping as to what was wrong with him. But Vergia smiled so sweetly at him, he forgot all about his confusion. She helped him to sit up, propping his pillow so that he should be perfectly comfortable. As she did so she came close to him, and a strand of her golden hair brushed his cheek. Her eyes met his, and Yonne felt again the spell of her beauty.

His hosts departed apparently satisfied that he was all right. He dressed hurriedly, determined to find out at once where he was. His mind was clear. He had a plan all worked out.

Yonne judged the time to be noon, for the sun was streaming into his room at a high angle. The air was cool and refreshing, and the twittering of birds came through the open windows. He felt in high spirits. Walking to the windows he noticed that his quarters were high above the ground in one of the multicolored turrets. He was able to gaze over the tops of the surrounding trees, and to see other turrets similar to the one he was in. Each turret was of some distinctive botanical pattern, each one craning its floral crest above the cluster of trees that hid the lower portions from view.

As far as he could see, quaint dwelling places like Bornabi's dotted the landscape, though always they were a goodly distance apart and surrounded by heavy foliage. Ripening fields and rich, profuse plant life showed plainly that nature was bountiful.

In every direction he noticed extensive wooded tracts. One of them especially caught his eye. Circular in shape and made up of trees of immense size, it seemed to be a part of the estate, being about a mile from the house and connected with it by narrow paths. The trees belonged to the pine family, and had tall, straight trunks and pointed crests. Their branches were thick-leaved, and pendulous, and they grew in an even, upward angle, like the branches of the cypress. They looked like giant spears piercing the sky. Swaying silently back and forth, high above the other foliage, there was something inspiring yet mournful about them. Their huge bulk cast a great shadow, and they seemed to be trying to extend themselves to yet greater heights, as though seeking vainly to unite the lowliness of their earthen bed with the tranquility of the sky above.

Yonne observed that the grove was accessible from four paths, and between them the land was covered with dense, almost impenetrable vegetation. Everything grew in wild profusion in this little jungle, the paths winding in irregular fashion, often turning completely back upon their course, or brushing the side of another, yet always remaining hidden from each other by the thick intervening foliage. Like streams groping their way through stubborn country toward a common goal, all the lanes advanced gradually towards the circle of pines. Singularly enough, they finally penetrated the center from the four points of the compass.

It was a queer piece of landscaping with an artistic purpose incomprehensible to Yonne.

As he studied the scene, a group of loud-chirping birds flew toward the turret and perched themselves on a ledge directly below his room. They were tiny creatures with crimson plumage and white heads. Yonne made a slight movement of his body, and they flew with a frightened twitter to a lower ledge. Presently they began to screech in great excitement. It was as though they had been startled by the presence of an enemy in the turret. One of them flew again to the window and peered boldly through it. Yonne tapped against the pane, wherupon the little fellow took flight, followed by the entire noisy crew. He could hear them screaming their protests until they were out of sight. He mused. Did these little creatures sense his strange origin —and resent it?

From the garden below came the sound of voices. Yonne saw Vergia coming toward the house with a young man. The two were walking arm-in-arm and chatting. He saw the man give Vergia a small, neatly wrapped package. On approaching the entrance to the house, he whispered something into her ear and she seemed pleased. He took her hands in his, their eyes met. He drew her close and kissed her full upon the lips. Yonne felt a pang of jealousy, then smiled at the presumptuousness of his feelings.

He watched them exchange a few more words then part, the man walking hurriedly down the road leading from the estate, she waving to him till he was out of sight. She remained standing at the doorway a moment as though undecided about something, then looked up toward Yonne's rooms. His heart skipped a beat. Could she be thinking of him? Again she glanced up. Then, with a quick decisive movement she walked hurriedly in the direction of the beach.

Yonne sat on the bed to analyze his surging feelings. He had just met this woman—hardly knew her more than by name—yet his fascination was intense! He felt even now a desire to rush after her, to be close to her. And there were the many things he wanted to find out. She could help him.

He set out and found her seated on a bench in a far corner of the garden. She seemed startled as he came suddenly upon her, and he too became confused. He began to stammer an apology again, and this time, despite the language barrier, she understood and smilingly invited him to sit down.

Yonne noticed she had opened her package. In it were some books, one of which containing undecipherable markings she smilingly offered him. He returned it with a shrug of futility. To his surprise, she thrust it back into his hand and nodded emphatically.

"For me?" he inquired, pointing to himself.

"Yes," she seemed to say, and nodded again.

He did not understand at once, then suddenly her meaning dawned on him. He was to study her language from these texts. She would teach him.

Something in Vergia's manner confirmed what was already disturbing him. As he stood there confused and speechless, she regarded him sympathetically, and extended her hand. He grasped it in a silent token of gratitude.

* * * * *

That night Yonne sat alone on the beach watching the stars as they moved imperceptibly across the sky. For hours he watched their silent procession. He waited for the moon to come along its accustomed course. But there was no moon. He observed the North Star and the motion of the familiar constellations—Ursa Major, Ursa Minor, Cassiopeia —with reference to that star. They gave their answer.

Not only did the constellations move in a completely new course, but the Polar star moved with them! The fixed point in the heavens had shifted wide of the earthly mark. Sidereal formations no longer rotated about the North Pole.

Unwilling to believe, Yonne sat mulling the evidence over in his mind.

His thoughts turned to the implications of the thing— this reality that he was actually upon another world! What would be the prospects of life upon this strange planet? What gulf in understanding would separate him, hopelessly, perhaps, from its inhabitants?

He felt misgivings crowd in upon his brain. There would be difficulties of customs, of habits, of mental outlook on all things. Yes, if it were true, there would be the delicate task of trying to convey to the people here his Earthly origin. Would they believe, or would they think him mad?

The idea itself was maddening. How had he gotten here, and how would he ever get back? A queer feeling came over him—a feeling that his Earthly existence would henceforth be but a shadowy memory, like the superhuman recollections of some tormented soul that remembers longingly the scenes of a former life to which it can never again return.

Yonne rested his tired eyes upon the water. A sharp wind blew up and it fanned the waves into angry white caps. The green, undulating body of the sea took on an ominous appearance under the dark sky and the faint light of the stars. It seemed like a living monster with a thousand gnashing teeth, heaving its bulging body in anger, ready to rush in upon him and to engulf him within its grasp.

He lifted his eyes again to heaven. All was quiet and serene there. The stars twinkled lazily. In the quiet and peace of their infinite magnitude he felt a sense of reassurance that all was well and that little did it matter what would become of his own insignificant bodily self.

III

Contrary to Yonne's misgivings, the weeks following his arrival on Vinibus proved to be delightful. Vergia and he met daily for his linguistic education. The language she taught him was common to all the people. It was called, "Vinibin," after the name of their planet, "Vinibus." The people themselves were known as "Vinibins," and they learned this universal tongue from early childhood together with their local and native one. Vergia told him it was used exclusively in all official and public transactions throughout Vinibus. Though remarkably expressive, it was noted for simplicity of structure. Yonne would listen to the sound of words and watch the movement of Vergia's lips as she related her enunciation to action and things themselves. Something in the manner of her instruction made the task simple and they made astonishingly fast progress.

In the afternoon Vergia always left the estate, and Yonne would not see her again until the following day. His growing attachment to her made him resent this separation, but the hours of solitude enabled him to concentrate upon the lessons. He would spend the afternoons on the beach, pacing up and down on the sand, like the ancient Demosthenes, shouting the more difficult Vinibin words above the sound of the waves.

The language lessons were indispensable. They became for Yonne the "open sesame" to the secrets of Vinibin phenomena. They bridged for him what seemed at first an insurmountable barrier, and he appreciated, as he never had before, the power of speech.

Once able to converse on even the simplest topics, he began to burn with curiosity for the answer to an obvious question.

"How did people live on this planet? How did their life compare with life on Earth?"

But before this tantalizing thing could be found out, another more pressing matter had to be disposed of: his own identity. How could he ever convey to these Vinibins the incredible fact of his Earthly origin without appearing downright insane?

Vergia brought up the subject herself at a moment when his mind was farthest from it. It happened after an especially difficult linguistic session. They were seated under a tropical shade tree, he reclining on the grass, she perched on a low branch that twisted downwards from the main trunk to the ground to form a natural seat. A light breeze played with the folds of her dress. A few stray sunbeams found their way through the thick-leafed tree to alight upon her gown and her hair. It was not a day for study, with the sun bright in the blue sky, and the air fragrant with the scent of growing things.

Yonne's eyes had been wandering more and more from the text to the lovely woman before him. Preoccupied with thoughts of her, he had been committing some absurd blunders in pronunciation. Vergia could not contain her amusement, and she burst into laughter.

"Why all this difficulty?" she asked with a chuckle.

"It's no use!" he declared slamming shut the book and throwing it upon the grass.

"Oh, you mustn't give up so easily" she protested playfully. "Try again."

Her soft brown eyes betrayed the slightest twinkle and

looked devastatingly into his. The breeze blew the sleeves of her dress back from her arm, and Yonne beheld her delicately curved shoulder.

He jumped to his feet. "Let's take a walk. The day is too beautiful for books."

Vergia smiled gaily and arose too. She took his arm, and they strolled towards the beach. When they came to the water's edge, the craft was discernable some few hundred yards away, nestling lazily like a great bird on the sand. Vergia had never alluded to it. As she saw it now her eyes sparkled; for a moment she said nothing, then she turned to him and spoke in a voice that was a bit tense.

"You have never told me anything of yourself, Yonne."

He squirmed. "You have never asked."

"Do you wish to keep it a secret?"

"No, of course not!"

He was eager to talk, but could not bring himself to it. Vergia looked puzzled.

"You seem uneasy."

"I am!" His vehemence made them both smile.

They walked again in silence. A breeze came in from the sea, and they sat on the beach, both knowing this was the moment they had been waiting for. Yonne picked up a handful of the clean sand and played aimlessly with it, letting the grains filter between his fingers as the wind scattered them evenly over the ground. He looked at Vergia.

"Well, what shall I tell you?"

She caught eagerly at his words. "Everything Yonne! Everything about yourself, your ship . . . your people.

Her eyes shone. But Yonne was still at a loss; how to say it without appearing ridiculous!

"Where do you think I came from?"

"I don't know. That is for you to say, Yonne."

"And what will you say when I tell you?"

She laughed. "You are funny. You want to know all the answers from me while it is I who ask the questions."

"Will you believe me," he continued doggedly, "if I tell you?"

Vergia turned to him in surprise. "Of course, I will. All Vinibins are——"

He interrupted nervously. "All right—here it is!"

He picked up a twig that had been washed up by the water, and looked for a smooth spot on the sand. Vergia watched him curiously.

"What are you going to do?"

"You will see."

He made a sweeping gesture toward the sky, then drew two circles on the sand. One he labeled "Earth" and the other, "Vinibus." With an inquiring glance at Vergia, he added a few markings to indicate familiar constellations. Not a word was spoken by either of them. Then slowly he moved the point of the twig across the sand, drawing a curved line from "Earth" to "Vinibus."

"This," he said with measured words, "is the path I travelled."

He watched the effect upon Vergia. In an instant she was upon her feet.

"Oh, then it is true!" she exclaimed.

"Yes . . . it is true," he stammered still trying to convince himself.

"Then we were right! We knew it!"

"You knew it?"

"All Vinibus knew it."

"You mean, you knew I came from Earth?"

"Yes!" Vergia gave a deep sigh. "So it has really happened!" She looked at him with wonder. "From the very beginning, Yonne, our people sought to explain your appearance here. They could not account for it in any other way."

Yonne gasped. To be so completely anticipated was more than he had bargained for. He was almost disappointed.

"But how could your people know?"

"They could not know for certain, Yonne. Ever since your arrival, however, some Vinibins whose judgment we most respect have held that you came from another planet. That was, in fact, my own first thought. But we could not be sure. Now, Yonne, you have confirmed it by your own words. Oh, it is marvelous!"

"Yes." He felt a sense of great relief come over him.

Vergia went on enthusiastically: "Why did you not tell me long ago?"

"Long ago?" he grinned. "Long ago we didn't talk to each other."

*   *   *   *   *

Yonne fully expected the news of his presence to bring great throngs of Vinibins to the estate, but nothing happened and no one came. When Vergia told Bornabi, he seemed deeply moved but said simply, "This is a wonderful thing, Sir Yonne." He always prefixed Yonne's name with this title of respect. "This is a great achievement, Sir Yonne!" That was all.

The next morning Yonne found that Bornabi had gone.

Vergia smiled archly across the breakfast table and answered his unspoken query. "He has gone on a matter of great importance." From the expression on her face, he knew that Bornabi's leaving had to do with the prospective role of the human visitor upon Vinibus. Indeed, he had already begun to speculate what that role might be. Through his pleasant relationship with Bornabi and Vergia, he now saw himself as a welcome guest upon Vinibus. All his former misgivings vanished. He would not be a stranger from another planet— an intruder to be misunderstood and possibly feared. In his mind's eye he was beginning to see himself perform an important service for Vinibins. He would be useful to them. He would build airships; he would bring to them the scientific knowledge of human beings, he would——

"How excited you must be!" declared Vergia.

"That's putting it mildly!" he replied with feeling.

"Of course!"

"Where has Bornabi gone?" he asked.

"To a neighboring province called Syrwalee."

"Syrwalee?"

"Yes."

"Does he go there often?"

"Oh, no." She grinned knowingly. "His present trip is most unusual." She held up two fingers. "Unusual on two counts: First, he is there about a festival."

"A festival?"

"Yes."

"And second?"

"About you!"

"Oh."

She smiled again, but this time there was something in her smile that brought back a flash of his old misgivings. Maybe, they were about to exhibit him before a curious Vinibin public . . . like some queer animal brought into captivity from another planet! He laughed nervously.

"Will you and Bornabi be there?" he asked trying to appear casual.

"Oh, yes, everybody will be there! The festival is held every year, but this will be the greatest of them all!"

"Hm! . . . will it be here in the country or in the, ah . . . " He groped for an expression to convey the idea of a city.

"A city?" Vergia looked at him dubiously. "What is that?"

"A city . . . surely, you have cities on Vinibus."

She shook her head blankly.

"You have no cities!" Yonne looked at her in surprise.

"No . . . What is a city?"

With a start, he realized this was the first time their conversations had truly touched upon a comparison of life upon Vinibus and Earth. With a kind of philosophical timidity, he proceeded to give Vergia a brief description of a city, then looked at her to see if she understood. Vergia shook her head.

"Never heard of one," she said.

"Never heard of a city? You mean all Vinibins still live on the land . . . on farms . . . in rural communities?"

"Yes, I believe so."

Yonne whistled. "Hm," he said meaningfully, "then you *do* have a long way to go yet, don't you?"

"Go where?" she asked.

He smiled. "Your people, I take it, have not yet reached the same stage that——" He decided not to finish what he had in mind.

He speculated as to the possible historical period in which these Vinibins might be living. The rural aspect of their society, he conjectured, suggested some stage equivalent to the close of our Middle Ages—though he wondered about this because he knew that human beings even then had made some progress towards an urban civilization. Still, he thought, further back in social evolution Vinibins surely cannot be, for there was much evidence of culture and refinement in both his hosts and in their surroundings. But, this alone was no criterion. He remembered the sophisticated civilizations of the ancient Romans and Greeks. And he remembered how much his first impression of Vinibus had reminded him of human antiquity.

While he pondered over this, Vergia was similarly struggling in her own mind with the idea of city life.

"It seems a most unusual arrangement," she said after

some silence. "I don't see how so many people can live in the small space you call a city. Why, if we tried that I believe we should have to live on top of one another!"

"That is just what we do," said Yonne laughingly.

"Really! . . . In airships?"

"Well, not exactly."

"But it doesn't sound possible."

"Oh, it is quite within possibility," he assured her. He was becoming confident now. "Your people will come to it in due time and by the same laws that brought us there a little sooner, perhaps, than you."

Vergia gazed upon him with wonder and admiration. "But now with you to advise us, Yonne," she said eagerly putting her hand upon his arm, "we shall circumvent the laws!"

He pressed her hand, the thrill of its touch adding to the joy that was in his heart. Vergia too was in a buoyant mood. She looked out and saw that the morning was a glorious one.

"Let us take a walk on the beach, Yonne."

"I'd love to," he said pleased at her desire to be with him. "I haven't really had a good look at things here."

"I'll show you around," she said. "We'll go a ways along the beach then come back through a lovely wooded path. It's my favorite walk."

Nothing could suit him better. He knew Vergia wanted to talk about many things that were on her mind, and he too was ready for an exchange of thoughts.

On the lawn outside, they were met by the once ferocious looking beast that had frightened him out of his wits the day he landed. It was really an affectionate little creature, and it loved to accompany them on their walks. It's name was "Kooklwucs," meaning pet. It had just been basking lazily in the sun and showed its joy by giving out a donkey-like bray and gamboling toward them, its ungainly legs and neck wriggling in the air. Then, in canine fashion, it got itself among their legs to be sure of receiving attention. Vergia petted it then sent it on ahead of them.

"I can see that Kooklwucs loves you," said Yonne.

"Can you?" She turned her face fully upon him.

"It could not do otherwise," he said. "You are so beautiful."

She laughed lightly and tossed her wavy hair in pleasure. She was especially pretty this morning, wearing a simple wash dress with puffed half sleeves and starched skirt that went to the knees. Yonne was struck with its similarity to the sort of dress girls wore on Earth. As a matter of fact, he found it hard to believe that he was no longer upon Earth and not at some delightful seaside resort with Vergia as his charming companion. For the first time he noticed how much everything really created the illusion of an Earthly setting: the brilliance of the sun, the blue of the sky, the whiteness of clouds; the glistening sea and the surf playing upon the shoreland; the cool ocean breeze blowing lightly across the countryside; the sparkling dew upon the grass, the leaves of trees, and the gossamer webs spun by Vinibin spiders before the light of day. Things grew and blossomed and wilted as on Earth, and familiar earthly creatures thrived everywhere.

As though divining his thoughts, Vergia asked, "Shall I introduce you to some of our Vinibin kin—our kin a few times removed?"

"I'd be delighted."

"All right!"

"Do they live here on the estate?" Yonne asked.

"Yes, along this wooded trail. Come I'll show you," and she took him by the hand down a narrow path leading from the shore. There was a screeching and twittering in one of the trees. "Ah, I hear one of them now. I shall introduce you." She imitated the sound, and presently a half dozen downy-furred rodents the size of chipmunks emerged from behind some roadside shrubbery.

"Your relations?" Yonne chuckled.

"Yes."

At first the little fellows looked furtively about, then, at the sight of Vergia, came out boldly. At her word they were all over her and Yonne. A friendly, playful lot, it was evident they were used to her visits.

"Tell the stranger, Man, your name," she coaxed one of them playfully as she gave Yonne its paw. The animal blinked its eyes comically and twittered with great to-do. "It is saying its name is "Speydi" and that it is a great friend of Vinibins. It is telling you, Yonne, that it likes to eat destructive insects and help keep our forests nice and clean." Yonne acknowledged the acquaintance, then Vergia shooed them away.

The path now led through the dense tropical growth Yonne had seen from the sleeping turret. Vergia showed him an odd, fernlike plant called, "Revoa." "Take a good look at the ground," she said, "and you will see how soft the Revoa has left it."

"It moves!" said Yonne in surprise.

"Yes, we call it the roaming Revoa because it creeps slowly along as the fibrous roots work ceaselessly in search of food."

"How unusual!"

"It too is a great little Vinibin helper. It leaves a fine, soft dirt in its path that is ideal for planting."

"What nice relatives you have," said Yonne. He spied a pale blue flower of delicate hue and reached out for it. He was about to pluck it when Vergia sprang to his side and

36

pulled him back with a start. He looked at her in surprise. "Eh, eh, I mustn't pick!" he declared with boyish guilt. But Vergia's face was white.

"Don't touch it!" she cried. "That's a Nefarl."

"Huh?"

"One prick from its thorns spells instant death."

Yonne recoiled. "What a nasty relative!" But he was plenty scared when he saw the long, sharp thorns. "Why do you keep it on the ground?"

"It must have sprung up overnight. The flower is rarely found away from its natural habitat and only in a few remote parts of Vinibus." She regarded Yonne thoughtfully. "You know what this means?" Her voice was dead serious.

"That I'm not safe out of your hands yet," he replied laughingly.

"No—there has been a violent typhoon somewhere on Vinibus. It has carried the pollen to extreme heights."

"And dropped one here?"

"Yes, thousands of miles away."

"What will you do about it?"

"Remove it, of course," she declared. "It certainly gave me a shock!"

"It almost liquidated me!"

She seemed to have to make an effort to regain her cheerfulness. At last she said, "I mustn't worry you about this, Yonne." She took his hand with forced gaiety, and they walked on. "Today, of all days, I want you to make more pleasant acquaintanceships."

She pointed out a large palm tree. "This is the 'Wahla' tree. You will have cause to be grateful to it, Yonne, when you travel in the torrid regions of Vinibus. It has a capacity for absorbing the hot, tropical air and giving off a magic coolness under its broad spreading leaves.

Yonne saw that the forest abounded with birds of all

37

shades and descriptions. He met again the tiny, bright colored "Daifili"—those impudent rascals who visited him in the sleeping turret. He saw tall, solemn looking cranes that stood on one leg, their heads buried in their plumage as though they hadn't an enemy to fear; and skylarks that perched on the uppermost branches of trees to sway gracefully in the breeze. But most interesting of all was a gray bird resembling our common sparrow. It was called the "Gylu," and beneath its drab feathers was a soulful little creature with a rare gift of song.

Often in days to come when Yonne would tramp these woods, he would listen for the song of the Gylu. At dusk the male called its mate, commencing in low, cooing tones. Gradually, the song rose in plaintive melody, then faded away. Again and again the call was repeated, each time more alluring to the loved one, until at last the appeal became irresistible. Then the female could be seen to dart from a nearby tree, the male following in pursuit. There would be a faint rustle in the leaves, a mingled twitter. The female, warm with the thrill of sex, could be heard to flutter about in mock attempt at flight; then silence, and the elemental consummation of love.

Even now Yonne was entranced by the song of the Gylu. Vergia watched him intently, a smile playing upon her lips.

"You like the Gylu?" she asked.

"Yes." He listened. "What a tender little creature!" Instinctively he drew closer to her. "There is something in its simple song . . . something that makes me feel at one with everything." As he turned to look at her, she said:

"I am glad you feel that way, Yonne." The tone in her voice bespoke deep satisfaction—satisfaction with something in him about which she seemed not to have been certain. She regarded him now with a kind of surety that seemed to say he had just been tested and found acceptable. The song of the Gylu had told her that.

Yonne felt a wistful, melancholic mood steal over him. "Why did you bring me here?" he asked.

"Because I wanted to talk to you."

"About the festival?"

"Yes."

"What do you call it?"

Vergia regarded him thoughtfully for a moment before answering. "The Kinship of All Living Things."

"Ahuh." He looked about smiling. "And you feel this is a fitting place."

"Yes. The holiday is dear to all Vinibins. Do you want to hear about it?"

"Of course."

"You have such a holiday on Earth?"

"I don't know. I don't think so."

"Strange," she said. "With us it is the basis of . . . of . . . well." She threw up her hands and laughed lightly at her inability to find the right words. She screwed up her face in perplexity. "Well, it is the beginning and end of every-thing."

"I am very curious," he said.

"Then, let's find a place to sit down."

"That suits me fine!" he declared. "I want to look at you!"

She seemed more ravishing than ever here in the rugged out-of-doors. He was falling in love with her. No doubt about it. He wanted to tell her. But there was still that blocking that came of a vague sense of dissimilarity, a realization that they were, after all, beings from different planets. Besides, she had never given him cause to believe that she shared his ardor, and this only increased his feelings of uncertainty.

"Here is a nice spot," said Vergia brightly. They had come to the end of the trail and out upon an open field. There was an old, gnarled tree at the edge of the forest, and again one of its branches was bent low to the ground as if deliberately to serve her gracious body by forming a natural seat for her. Yonne helped her on to it and sat on the grass beside her.

It was refreshingly cool in the shade, and they could overlook the sunlit field hemmed in by black forest. The color contrast between field and woods, and the sweet scent of growing things gave them a feeling of well being. Vergia saw that Yonne was glad. As she sat there beside him, she swung her shapely legs. They brushed against him, and he quickened at their touch. Irresistibly, his eyes followed their graceful lines into the thin folds of her dress. For a moment their eyes met, but it was for a moment only. Then Vergia gazed out over the meadow and gave a sigh of pleasure. She stretched out her arms as if to embrace the Universe.

"Ah!" she cried, "it is good to be alive—to sense the throbbing and bursting of kindred living things all striving for the ecstasy of life and light."

"Which brings us back to the subject!" observed Yonne with a mischievous protest in his voice.

"Yes," she said.

"Tell me all about it." He leaned forward and drew up his legs, clasping them with his arms like a little boy ready to hear a story.

It was to be a story, but one for which he was not quite prepared!

"The holiday starts in two days," said Vergia, "and it reaffirms our faith in the unity of all life, in the equality of all living things, from the lowliest to the highest, from the nearest to the farthest. Many years ago we did not know this basic truth, and Vinibins despaired of living! But now, for nearly a thousand years, we have commemorated its discovery. It is a concept that permeates the very details of our daily affairs."

"Your religion?" he asked, but Veriga shook her head.

"We Vinibins dedicate this time to the multitudinous forms of life about us: to friend and foe; to beast and insect; to every creeping thing both large and small; to plant and flower; to all the struggling host of beings whose destiny we Vinibins hold in the hollow of our hand." She stopped to look inquiringly at her human visitor.

"Go on," he said.

"On this occasion, Yonne, we seek to atone for the immeasurable harm we commit against their kind in the unending and oft inscrutable struggle for life."

There was a morbid note in her words that came as a shock to Yonne. He started to express his astonishment but decided upon silence. Vergia went on with her description of the somber holiday:

"The Kinship of All Living Things gives expression to our awareness that the Vinibin species is the deadliest of all contenders, the most menacing to the life and well-being of all other living forms. And, yet, at this time, we also voice our faith in the deeper and reconciling meaning in this struggle, a reconciliation that we find in the antinomy of life and death that binds all unlike species in an everlasting and a universal kinship."

Vergia paused again to scrutinize him. His feeling of discomfort still obsessed him, but he hung on her words.

"Go on."

"There is no more," she replied simply.

"But the Festival? Is it all so sad?"

Vergia laughed. "Of course not. There is merriment too— but that comes at the end. The holidays last seven days.

They begin with 'All Beings Day' when children make pilgrimages into the country and the forest to place nests for birds and small animals, and to plant growing things. Then comes the 'Song of Songs' when we pay tribute to all the bards, living and dead, that are dear to the hearts of Vinibins."

"That sounds much better," he said.

She looked at him wistfully. "Do your people on Earth sing often?"

"Oh yes!" he said, glad to be on familiar ground. "We have our choruses and choirs and operas, and many other kinds of music too."

"Ah, that is good." She said it as though she had half expected a different answer. "Singing plays a large part in the activities of the Kinship of All Things, especially on the last day. Then, we bring the observances to a close in a festive spirit. The final celebration is called the 'Dance of Love.' I think you will like that." She smiled, and her face became its wholesome, lovely self again.

Yonne gave a sigh of relief, but he wasn't at all sure he liked this part of Vinibin temperament.

"Oh, there is something else," she said, then quickly put her hand to her lips.

"What?"

"I'm sorry. You must wait till Bornabi comes back." She looked contrite.

"But it's about Bornabi that I am most curious," protested Yonne.

Vergia grinned. "I know, so am I!"

They were interrupted by the sound of a distant carillon announcing the time of day when Vergia generally had to leave the estate. "Come," she said cheerfully but decisively, "you will learn soon enough."

"Well, if that isn't just like a woman!" exclaimed Yonne.

"Vinibus or Earth—it's all the same!"

"What do you mean?"

"You start something just to get a man awfully curious—then you leave him dangling in mid-air!"

For an answer, Vergia laughed heartily. She took his hand, and they started across the field. They followed a short cut through the woods, and though Yonne wanted badly to continue the conversation, he realized from Vergia's manner that he was to ask no further questions, that perhaps she didn't know the answer—or wasn't permitted to tell it if she knew!

IV

That afternoon Yonne started for the beach to look after the plane, a duty he performed religiously every day, on the assumption that if he were destined to bring the art of flying to Vinibus, he had better have an eye for the safety of the craft.

There was really no need for concern, for Vinibins had already constructed a sturdy hangar over it. However, he always tinkered with the parts, checking everything carefully to be sure all was well.

Today, his mind was not on the plane. He was restless. Vergia's description of the forthcoming holiday bothered him. Bornabi's absence made him uneasy too. He began to imagine all kinds of weird things again that these Vinibins might have in store for him.

He decided a brisk walk along the beach would be a good tonic for his troubled thoughts. Soon he came to a place where the low trees along the shore projected out into the sea some few hundred yards hiding from view what was on the other side. As he approached, his ear caught the sound of music, and he could hear a woman's voice of fine quality accompanied by a harp. The strains came from the trees, but as these grew close together, he could see no one. He made his way through the underbrush and, to his surprise, saw Vergia and the Vinibin with whom she had been that first morning when he saw them from the sleeping turret. He remembered with a twinge of feeling the kiss the stranger had given her.

Jealous and dejected because she had not told him about this meeting, he started to turn back, but curiosity held him. He waited. They were at the water's edge, the stranger seated at the harp, she standing beside him. She began another song, the melody, a pastoral one, delicate and wistful, such as Mozart or Schubert might have written. She sang it beautifully, and the stranger played the harp with the ease of a master. Gently, briskly, his fingers moved over the strings; now angrily, like the claws of a tiger, now caressingly with a lingering tenderness. Yonne listened, and another song followed, this one light and airy and swift moving, like some playful scherzo depicting the dance of elves or wood nymphs. The voice came clear and lyrical. The harp sounded like distant rippling water and seemed to unite with the rhythmic drone of the surf upon the beach.

He had to admit to himself that they made an enchanting picture, Vergia dressed in the flowing gown which she had worn when he first met her on the beach; the stranger, in the colorful Vinibin knee breeches, shirt and sandals. He listened a while longer then returned moodily to the house. They did not return.

Yes, he was jealous—and hurt. He pondered the relationship of the two and became more despondent than ever.

44

The emotional tension of the last few weeks and of what was yet to happen to him did not help his low spirits any. The suspense kept him in a perpetual state of apprehension and he was forever wavering between fits of elation and despair. Now he was at the bottom again. Sullen thoughts possessed him, and he brooded about his uncertain role in this strange world.

Why was he being kept here all alone anyway? Were these Vinibins really glad he was here or were they suspicious of him—suspicious that he might have come as the advance scout of a superior Earthly race bent on conquest or some other ill mission? Did they keep him in this secluded retreat, not as a privileged guest, but as a virtual prisoner, until they could learn more about his motives? This all could be so; the gracious hospitality might be but a cloak.

Dusk began to fall, then night. A sharp drop in temperature made him feel cold and miserable. A fresh breeze blew up from the ocean, and it rustled through the leaves making them shiver as though they too were chilled and uncomfortable. With an utter sense of loneliness, he betook himself to the plane, the one familiar object, the haven of refuge for all his troubled moments.

* * * * *

He spent the night restlessly curled up in the fuselage of the plane and rose at dawn. Hurrying to the house he was surprised to find Vergia already up and about. She was at work in one of the gardens examining a young Wahla tree that looked withered and ailing.

"Ah, my dear Yonne!" she cried. "It is good to see you out so soon. You are beginning to get used to our customs."

"They are infectious," he said, forgetting his despondency at the mere sight of her. "I can no longer sleep after dawn."

45

"No need to, Yonne. Early morning is the best part of the day."

"How early?" He asked with a wry face as he looked up at the still half-gray sky just being illuminated by the first rays of the sun.

Vergia shrugged her shoulders. "We are up with the birds, Yonne, and sometimes before. That is the way of life on Vinibus."

"A good habit if it agrees with you," he replied.

"Ah, but it does. Why shouldn't it?"

"It seems to." He gazed at her trim figure. "You Vinibins manage to look well with precious little sleep."

"Oh, I think we do quite well on sleep and rest, Yonne. There is the good old Vinibin rule: 'Early to bed and up with the birds.'"

He chuckled. "The old adage seldom adhered to. We have it on Earth too."

Vergia looked up from her work and regarded him earnestly. "But we Vinibins *do* observe it."

"Strictly?" he said with playful skepticism. "Never out late nights? Never that awful feeling the morning after?"

She shook her head in a genuinely puzzled manner, then said:

"Sometimes you say the queerest things, Yonne. I'm afraid I don't understand your meaning."

"Well," he declared, "sometimes you puzzle me too! That's to be expected, though, isn't it, between persons of slightly different social backgrounds?" He laughed. "Perhaps, you Vinibins keep closer to the straight and narrow path than we."

"What path is that?"

"The path from which we humans sometimes wander for a lark after a hard day's work."

"Hm!" Vergia looked thoughtful.

46

"Maybe, a little affair of the heart?" He felt the pang of anger returning as he thought of the young Vinibin. He pretended to be facetious but was probing her. She answered blandly by repeating his words in the form of a question:

"Affair of the heart?"

"Love affair."

She inclined her head and looked amused. "Why, yes, of course," she said, "all Vinibin girls have love affairs."

He winced.

"But why do you say after a hard day's work?" she asked, and her look became quizzical again.

"People on Vinibus work—don't they?" The thought seemed obvious, yet her blank stare made him wonder. "I mean . . . well, surely, you all have to work here . . . you don't just . . . " He was having trouble trying to convey a simple human term.

Vergia smiled curiously. "Let's talk about this more later—after we have had breakfast," she said indulgently. "Then you can clear up what you are trying to tell me. Right now I want you to meet a guest."

"Bornabi?" he asked eagerly.

"No." Her eyes twinkled. "Someone else."

As she spoke, the young Vinibin came out of the house. Seeing Yonne, he stopped suddenly with a look of anxiety. Vergia hurried forward to greet him.

"Come, Eroscheen, you will now meet the stranger, Man!" She took him by the arm and turned to Yonne. "Yonne, I want you to meet my brother, Eroscheen."

Brother? Yonne rushed forward to grasp his hand. "I am so happy to meet you!"

The Vinibin's face relaxed at this enthusiastic reception. He bowed graciously. "I am happy to meet you, too, Sir Yonne." Like Bornabi, he prefixed Yonne's name with this honorary title.

They stood silent for a moment. Vergia turned again to her brother.

"Had you come any other time, Eroscheen, you would not have found Yonne up so early. He is adopting Vinibin customs."

"When on Vinibus, do as Vinibins do," Yonne said with a chuckle.

"No!" broke in Eroscheen eagerly. "We Vinibins hope soon to do as Humans do on Earth." He regarded Yonne with open reverence and his intelligent and sensitive face showed such excitement that Yonne had to repress a smile. He was unmistakably handsome, with a boyish freshness and modesty. Physically well developed, tall and muscular, he would have made a fine masculine impression in any Earthly setting. And he was clearly overwhelmed by the daring adventure of the human visitor.

"Eroscheen is an authority on meteorology," said Vergia.

"I see—and interested in aeronautics."

"Yes!" said Eroscheen with fervor.

"Then you and I should get along well together," quipped Yonne good-humoredly.

"I shall do anything you say, Sir Yonne, perform any task you ask!" With a worshipful expression he hastened to add, "That is, anything *you* think I can do."

Yonne promised he would be the first Vinibin to learn to fly, and Eroscheen murmured his gratitude.

They entered the house and sat down to breakfast. Throughout the meal, Eroscheen gazed raptly at his hero from Earth. Ardently as he may have wished to ply him with questions about his adventure, he kept his silence. It was as though he regarded the subject too sacred to be reduced to mere conversation. Vergia brought it down to mentionable aspects.

48

"Eroscheen will be happy to study flying as soon as you are ready for him, Yonne."

"The sooner the better," replied Yonne.

"Why not today?" cried Eroscheen.

"Of course!" But Yonne had to correct himself. "No, we shall have to wait." He thought of the meager supply of fuel left in the tank. If Vinibins were as retarded scientifically as he suspected they were, he knew replacement would be problematical. "You will have to give me time to check the plane's requirements." he said.

Eroscheen was crestfallen, but he was content to wait. After the meal, he excused himself. Bowing with outward formality, but his eyes sparkling with boyish excitement, he left the room.

"A splendid young man," said Yonne after he had gone.

"Vinibin," she corrected laughingly.

"Vinibin, of course."

She was eager to talk about him. "You will find Eroscheen quite different from me."

"I like you as you are."

She avoided his glance but he noticed she was pleased.

"You say he is a meteorologist?"

"Yes. He is attached to the Weather Bureau at Syrwalee, and he enjoys it immensely."

"An accomplished person, indeed," said Yonne. "He is a fine musician too."

"Yes, a fine harpist." She stopped and looked suddenly at him. "How did you know?"

Yonne confessed his eavesdropping. "I did not know he was your brother," he said guiltily.

"Who did you think he was?"

"Your——"

As he flushed, Vergia observed him. She played aimlessly

with her water glass. "I shall be going away with him tomorrow," she said.

"Tomorrow!" Yonne's face fell.

"To Syrwalee—to sing at the 'Song of Songs.' He will accompany me."

"How long will you be gone?"

"Just one day."

"Oh—that's better!"

She smiled.

"Even so, I shall miss you."

"Thank you."

"And when do I——"

"Go out among our people?" she said finishing the sentence for him.

"Yes."

"Soon, I hope. You will participate in the festival."

"I?"

"Yes—that is why Bornabi is now at Syrwalee."

Yonne nodded. Despite his curiosity he decided against further questioning. He would await developments with Bornabi's return. He returned to Vergia's singing.

"When you come back, will you sing for me?"

"Gladly."

"And Eroscheen . . . will he return too?"

"Perhaps. But he may be detained on other musical assignments." In a gay but confidential tone she added: "Eroscheen just detested playing the harp when he first began to study it. He said he much preferred to do bricklaying all the year round!"

"Bricklaying?" asked Yonne in amazement. "Is he a bricklayer? I thought you just said——"

"Yes," she answered without waiting for him to finish, "and a fine craftsman he is, too."

50

"A bricklayer and harpist? What a rare combination! And a meteorologist, too?"

Vergia regarded him a bit perplexed. Unconsciously they were making comparisons again of customs on Earth and Vinibus—and getting mixed up. "It is not rare, is it?" she said. "I saw his talents and I just would not let him give up the harp. Now he is glad that I prodded him on."

"You have done well by him!" declared Yonne. "It would have been a pity to have wasted such artistic ability on mere manual labor."

Vergia laughed. "You are jesting again, Yonne!"

"No, I am serious."

"But he would not be wasting his time, would he?" She looked inquiringly into his eyes. Yonne held up his hand and grinned.

"Wait!—we're on dangerous ground again!"

"Dangerous?—for the Man who dared the limitless space of the cosmos?" She teased him, but he refused to answer. Instead, he rose and walked towards the door shaking his head. "Where are you going?" she asked.

"For a walk in the air—to let the breeze clear some mental cobwebs. I'm in a fog again."

"So am I," she replied, and they both laughed. "Come, let me walk with you," she said taking his arm and grinning slyly.

"Where to?"

"To meet Bornabi."

"Bornabi!"

"He will be here soon."

"Well!" cried Yonne excitedly, "What are we waiting for?"

They hurried across the field to the edge of the grounds. With a nervous laugh, Vergia urged him to go faster.

"Why should *you* be upset?" he asked curiously.

"Because—I want everything to turn out all right."

"Could it turn out bad?"

"Not bad, but——" For the rest she squeezed his arm reassuringly, and they walked on in silence.

They came to a winding road arched by thick, leafy trees. They were on high ground and could see it extend for miles over hill and into valley, disappearing behind wooded tracts then emerging again, the leafy branches stirring slightly in the breeze like the downy fur of some giant green caterpillar crawling lazily over the country.

"He will come along here," said Vergia.

They had not gone far when they saw Bornabi trudging along leisurely at a bend in the road. When he saw them he waved excitedly and quickened his pace. The round, ruddy face beamed, and the small eyes danced.

"Sir Yonne!" he cried as he came upon them. "I have great news!"

"Tell us," said Vergia impatiently.

He rubbed his hands and chuckled. He seemed to enjoy keeping them in suspense.

"Ah, Sir Yonne, your coming means so much to us!"

Yonne tried to appear casual.

"Young and old alike, Vinibins are bursting with a desire to see you, inspired by the knowledge of your great achievement."

"They have let me peculiarly alone," said Yonne.

"Of course. Only complete rest and care saved you."

"Saved me?"

"Your illness—or don't you realize how sick you were? We feared for your life."

Yonne gasped in astonishment.

"You were a brave man," went on Bornabi, "to have dared the limitless vistas of interplanetary space! And an incredibly strong one to have survived it." His round face broke into a smile. "But, now you are hale and hearty again. You must have chafed under the confinement here."

Yonne groped for words. So that was it!—the reason for his seeming incarceration in Bornabi's home.

"How can I ever thank you both!" he burst out with gratitude.

"Not a word of it!" declared Bornabi, jovially waving aside the remark. "Let's get to the important news."

"Yes!" said Vergia excitedly. "Will Yonne go to the Eternal Circle?"

"He will."

"Wonderful!" She took Yonne's hands and looked at him with radiant face while he stared perplexedly.

"Tell him, Bornabi!" she said laughing at his dumb expression.

They walked back toward the house, arm in arm, Bornabi in the middle, Vergia and Yonne on either side.

"Tomorrow," began Bornabi, "starts the greatest of all Vinibin holidays—the Kinship of All Living Things."

"I know—Vergia has already told me."

"Ah, that is good. Then I can come directly to the point. During these holidays we hold meetings called Eternal Circles. They are the most important gatherings upon Vinibus, and only our foremost leaders attend. You, Sir Yonne, are to be present."

"I?—but I am not one of your leaders."

"You are jesting, Sir Yonne. You are more than one of our leaders."

"To be chosen to an Eternal Circle," broke in Vergia, "is the highest tribute ever to be bestowed upon a Vinibin. Only Vinibins who have performed outstanding service attend."

"So why me?" insisted Yonne doggedly. "I'm not a Vinibin, and I've performed no great Vinibin service."

"You have blazed a trail between two worlds," said Vergia. "By your heroic act, you have shown us that kinship between living things is infinite, extending to the very limits of the Universe."

"Yes," said Bornabi, "it is for this that we honor you, and beg you to come."

Yonne was confused and flattered.

"Besides," said Vergia, "the Eternal Circle will be a wonderful way for you to make your first contacts upon Vinibus. Afterwards, you will be able to visit all our lands."

"Well," he conceded laughingly, "putting it that way sounds convincing."

"Then you will attend?" they both exclaimed.

"I shall be delighted to."

"Good! In two days one of the Eternal Circles will meet here at the Cypress Grove," said Bornabi. "It is my great privilege this year to have been chosen as a Chieftain of the local province of 'Quiloth.' Three other such meetings will take place on Vinibus. They are the highest councils of the land, and they are carried on in strict seclusion."

Yonne nodded his interest, as Bornabi continued: "The Eternal Circles form the basis of Vinibin activity in all our endeavors—in Education, Production, Recreation, Aesthetics, Ethics. Each year we bring together there the latest knowledge available to Vinibinkind."

Into his face came a wistful look. "Do you see, then, Sir Yonne, why it is remarkable that you should have come to us from Earth on the eve of this great celebration?"

Yonne saw the coincidence and it gave him an increased sense of the importance of his role upon Vinibus. Bornabi was eager to explain.

"You are a messenger from another world, Sir Yonne, bringing to us the supreme testimony of the unity of life." He raised his hands solemnly toward heaven; there was a tone of deep conviction in his voice, an eloquence of gesture that was infectious.

Yonne felt the spell of his lofty words.

"It *is* an amazing coincidence!" he declared.

"A marvelous coincidence!" said Bornabi.

*   *   *   *   *

At sunset he and Bornabi went for a stroll along the beach. The air was mild and pleasant. Bornabi linked his arm into Yonne's, and they walked in silence, each lost in thoughts of the coming event.

Dusk was falling, and a somber gray fused the sea and sky into one. More and more Yonne felt a compelling urge about the happenings of the last few hours. Suddenly, he fathomed a new meaning in all that had transpired. A great idea took hold of him, an idea yet vague and uncertain, but strong, tumultuous . . . fomenting!

He glanced out over the ocean. In its vast expanse he saw reflected something of the depth of Bornabi's words, something of the broad motif of what Vergia had been telling him about this occasion.

As night came on, countless stars were mirrored on the liquid surface of the sea. How infinitely large was this cosmic panorama in contrast to his own small vision! He looked up and saw one lone star appear on the eastern horizon. It shone with unequalled brilliance. He knew that star; he knew it well, and gazed upon it, and felt a yearning for its familiar scenes.

Bornabi saw the star too, and understood.

They spoke not a word, but linked their arms more firmly, the human being and the Vinibin, strolling side by side along a shore of Vinibus!

V

The giant cypress trees stood ominously against the dull sky. They were like some black massive things shot directly from the bowels of Vinibus.

This was the day the Chieftains were to arrive. It was "All Beings Day," and Vinibin children were going to make pilgrimages into the forests.

The morning was warm and grey. A slight fog lay over the fields and the air was heavy with impending rain. There was a stillness over all things as in a churchyard.

"An appropriate setting," thought Yonne.

He wondered what Vergia was doing. Praying, perhaps? He wondered if Vinibins prayed. That they were a deeply religious people seemed evident. Bornabi's remarks of the previous day had sounded almost ecclesiastical in their phrasing.

Yonne was wearing the characteristic costume of the local province of Quiloth, with its loose flowing, silken blouse of yellow gold, its red and black knee breeches, and its brown ankle socks and sandals. His face and thighs were tanned by the Vinibusian sun. The knowledge that, outwardly at least, he looked like a Vinibin, gave him a satisfying feeling of "belonging."

About noon things began to happen. The surrounding country hitherto void of population now teemed with colorfully garbed children and adults. The winding roads and neighboring fields became dotted with groups of Vinibins all making their way toward Bornabi's estate. There was a blare of trumpets.

"The Chieftains are coming!" cried Bornabi. Vergia and Eroscheen came running out of the house. "The Chieftains! Let us go to meet them"

Bornabi linked his arm into Yonne's, as was his custom and, with Vergia and Eroscheen following, they hurried to the edge of the grounds. From all directions came Vinibins. Like so many gaily costumed jacks-in-boxes, they bobbed up from all places.

"Here come the Chieftains!" was the common, joyous cry.

At the head of the road whence Bornabi had returned from Syrwalee, they waited for the arrival of the noted guests. Children were romping and playing in the grass. All eyes were strained for sight of the Chieftains. Suddenly, a great shout went up from the crowd.

"Here they come!"

Yonne had looked forward to seeing a stately entourage. Instead, he saw four Vinibins come marching down the road by themselves, blowing lustily on trumpets, like a troupe of country musicians.

"The Chieftains?" he asked incredulously.

"Yes." said Bornabi. "Ah, it is great to see them."

Yonne almost burst out laughing. What a comical picture they made—the most celebrated Vinibins of the time trudging along the road and blowing on queer-shaped instruments to arouse the countryside!

The assembled Vinibins gave a rousing cheer as the visitors came into view. Bornabi was waving frantically, and when the Chieftains saw him they stopped playing right in the middle of their tune and ran joyfully towards him. The crowd made a big circle for them as each one in turn greeted and embraced Bornabi. Then the chieftains turned to the populace and bowed in acknowledgment of their welcome.

The din of the reception subsided, and Bornabi bade for silence. Without warning to Yonne, he did an unexpected thing. He disclosed Yonne's identity to the multitude.

"Fellow Vinibins," he said, "it is with unprecedented honor that I now introduce to you the most famous and discussed person on all Vinibus—the stranger, Man, Sir Yonne!"

There was a sepulchral silence. All eyes were turned to Yonne, The crowd was awe-stricken. Then suddenly, with one accord, they regained their voices, and welcomed him with lusty cheers such as they had given their Chieftains:

"Hail, Stranger, Man! Hail! Hail!"

Each Chieftain presented himself to Yonne. Instantly the carefree, happy atmosphere was restored. No one seemed to take further notice of him, as if by common understanding, and the simple ceremonies of receiving the Chieftains were resumed.

Now began the march back to the estate. The four Chieftains, blowing their tuneful trumpets, took the lead. It was a joyful crowd. Some began to sing, others laughed and chatted. The whole procession looked more like the homecoming of a group of picnickers led by the village band, than a reception of Vinibin notables. As they walked back to the house, Bornabi told Yonne something of his celebrated guests.

First and foremost he pointed out Ehduaart, a short, rolypoly little Vinibin of middle age. He was bald except for spare tufts of curly, sand-colored hair that grew in a thin fringe above the ears and along the back of the neck. Like Bornabi, he had a ruddy face, and it was round and shining like the face of a Polish peasant. His eyes were small and sparkling, and they seemed forever to be laughing. Though he looked like something out of a picture book, appearances were deceiving.

"Ehduaart is a great Vinibin leader," said Bornabi. "Mentally, he is cold and deliberate, and he can be depended upon to drive straight to the core of a knotty problem. It is for this quality mainly that he holds the high position of 'Chieftain of Production' of our neighboring Syrwalee province."

"For all his importance, he seems a most amiable fellow," ventured Yonne.

"Ah, yes," said Bornabi, "but underneath you will always find the dynamic, relentless mind, the cold analyst, the leader of Vinibins. Of all the Chieftains, Ehduaart is the most honored."

Walking beside Ehduaart, was Tsubandi, the youngest member of the group. A Vinibin of about 30 years of age, he looked terribly serious playing a little reed instrument that resembled an oboe. He stood fully six feet tall and had Mongolian features—yellowish complexion, straight, black hair, broad face, small nose, prominent cheek bones, and narrow, almond-shaped eyes. He was wiry and had quick, rather tense mannerisms.

"Tsubandi is a Vinibin of few words," said Bornabi, "but he can speak with conviction and eloquence in defense of a point. He is a dreamer and often speaks beyond the spiritual horizon of the present. But Vinibins love him for his creative faculty. They have made him 'Chieftain of Education' of his province."

Yonne noticed one member was a woman—a Negress of perhaps thirty-five years of age and striking appearance. She was beautiful, and she carried herself with superlative grace. Her face was not the pure Negroid type, but reminded one of the soft, well-proportioned lines of the Negro of mixed lineage. Her name was Luannah. Tall and slender, she had a rhythmic grace that accentuated bodily curve and symmetry. Her eyes were large and soft, and they had a dash of brilliance, the more alluring by virtue of their setting in the dark skin. Her hair, a rich black, was parted in the middle, tightly combed and twisted into two knots at the sides of her head. Her traveling attire consisted of loose silken slacks over which was worn a kind of hostess coat, both of black material designed in maroon, white and silver.

On first meeting Luannah, Bornabi embraced her, a little more eagerly, thought Yonne, than he had the male members. She gave him a pleased glance out of her large flashing eyes. Vergia looked at Yonne and grinned. "Of all his paramours," she whispered, "Luannah is still his favorite."

"Is she a Chieftain too?" he asked.

"Oh, yes—and lest you get any mistaken ideas," she added good-humoredly, "she is renowned not for her feminine charm, but for the distinguished services she has rendered to Vinibins." His amazement was complete when she said:

"Luannah has won fame in the field of Ethics and Knitting!"

But this was not a time to ask questions. He listened to Bornabi tell about the fourth Chieftain, a Vinibin of fair complexion and Herculean stature. His name was Knisslig. and he came from a distant polar province. He presented a picture of bodily strength. His hands were large, and his arms, bronzed and sinewy. He bore himself erect, and his head was held high on his broad shoulders. Knisslig had golden, wavy hair, and a face of chiseled marble.

In the great frame of this blond northerner, there dwelt a modest and lovable person. Knisslig's frank, kindly eyes and his warm smile disclosed an affectionate nature. Something simple and loyal emanated from his personality. Yonne learned that he was a bosom friend of Bornabi, and he could well understand the reason.

Knisslig was "Chieftain of Recreation" of his province.

With a smile of pride Vergia said to her father: "And don't forget to tell Yonne about yourself." She leaned on Bornabi's arm and regarded him affectionately. "Tell Yonne about the field that you will represent at the Eternal Circle."

"It is Aesthetics," said Bornabi, "and it forms one of the five major fields of Vinibin activity. It relates to a habit of life, an objective towards which all other endeavor is fashioned. For Vinibins, Aesthetics is the 'Art of Living Well.'"

*   *   *   *   *

Now, all this was a rather new and heavy mental diet for Yonne who had all his life nourished little on abstract ideas. But he was intensely curious and determined to learn what these Vinibin things were all about.

The party arrived at Bornabi's home. After much well-wishing and more exchange of greetings, the resident Vinibins dispersed and the visiting Chieftains were invited to a sumptuous meal, served on a long, rough-hewn table in one of the rustic chambers of Bornabi's home.

Vinibins were no meat eaters. But they had developed a fine art of preparing well-balanced and tasteful dishes made of animal and vegetable products. Steaming platters of these were on the table. Sea food was served in abundance, and everyone ate of a crisp, whole-grained bread. There were many kinds of fresh baked sweets, cakes, fruits, and nuts. Wines and fruit juices flowed freely for all the guests and were served in large mugs of grotesque design. It was a feast such as would have tickled the palate of any Earthly epicure.

Just how, when and by whom all the food had been prepared, Yonne did not know, for on this occasion as on others, he found everything ready when he arrived. There were no butlers or maids or cooks about the place. For the first time he was aware of this. With characteristic youthful preoccupation, he had never given a thought to this domestic detail. He decided he would ask Vergia at the very next opportunity.

Without formality and with great gusto, each guest fell to according to his likes. A jovial, hearty spirit prevailed. As Yonne looked about the spacious room with its tree colonnades and rough-hewn but artistic furniture, and then at the cheerful guests in their picturesque costumes, he was strangely affected by the entire setting. There was a primitive touch to the atmosphere, an animalistic exuberance and a peasant-like simplicity quite out of keeping with the otherwise refined character of the assembled guests. The queer fusion of peasant hardihood in the outward appearances of this scene, and of inner refinement in the characters themselves, made a striking impression on his mind.

Of course, he as the visitor from Earth, was the center of interest. After he had told them as best he could the vague facts of his arrival (which his imagination colored to a pardonable extent so as not to show him as quite the victim of the inexplicable forces that he really was), the conversation turned to affairs upon Vinibus. At once there was the old difficulty—the same blocking and confusion that had confronted him and Vergia, only this time it was much worse! Although the discussion was directed for his special benefit, and everyone talked in Vinibin, the Chieftains found it virtually impossible to carry on an intelligent conversation with him.

Things started out well enough, but after the first few simple exchanges of thought, there ensued a painful silence. No matter how hard the Chieftains tried, Yonne was unable to follow even the most trivial situations. Their world of experience was simply not his, and his not theirs. Vinibin anecdotes and jests called forth laughter from Vinibins, but he had to disentangle everything like a Chinese puzzle.

Yonne now realized how carefully and adroitly Vergia had been coaching their own conversations so that he could adapt simple human values to those upon Vinibus. He was not of a philosophical bent of mind, but this newest episode set him to thinking on some fundamental things: Here he was, a human being of normal adult intelligence, unable to find in the exchange of common, everyday Vinibin occurrences a single peg upon which to fasten his own understanding of them. Nor was he able to impart any of his own background to these good Vinibins. It startled him. With shocking awareness he divined something of the utter provincialism of all thought—Human and Vinibin; its incompleteness to an absurd degree. He saw, as never before, that what *is*, is only so for us—for them; that it is but a passing phase, a fragmentary piece in an infinitesimal corner of existence—nothing final, or sacred, or all-embracing.

As he sat there trying vainly to enter into the Vinibin spirit of conviviality, he continued to be obsessed with the deeper implications of his predicament: How stupidly, he thought, do we struggle to retain for eternity what has been created for a moment; how we cherish and idolize what has been established in our own little minds and in our own little ways of life, as though it were of universal import, like some fixed reality for all time and for all peoples! How diligently we do this, and, on occasion, with what appalling conceit, and with what colossal stupidity!

Luannah saw the worried look on Yonne's face. She caught everyone's attention with a question.

"How shall we go about the Eternal Circle, tomorrow?" she asked. "This is important now that Sir Yonne will be our honored guest."

"A good question," agreed Tsubandi, keenly aware as were all the others of the dilemma confronting them and the visitor from Earth. "We have invited Sir Yonne here to participate; we owe it to him to plan the sessions in accordance with his need rather than ours."

"What do you suggest?" asked Ehduaart.

Tsubandi thought hard and dug his hands into his thick, black hair.

"Please," said Yonne quickly, "don't disrupt your regular business for me."

"Oh, yes," said Ehduaart with calm decisiveness. "Tsubandi is right. We must find a way."

"We certainly must!" came from the others.

"I have it!" cried Tsubandi, but immediately he said, "No, no . . . it won't do."

"Tell us; maybe it will help," urged Ehduaart. Tsubandi hesitated.

"Out with it!" said Knisslig jovially.

"Well, said Tsubandi, looking dubiously at the others, "I propose we dispense with the usual proceedings, and let Sir Yonne tell us about the manner of life upon Earth. What could be of greater interest to Vinibins than—" But Tsubandi got no further. His words were greeted by an outburst of disapproval.

"For shame!" cried Bornabi.

"I am surprised at you!" said Ehduaart.

"A fine plan!" broke in Knisslig scornfully. "We invite our Earthly guest, Sir Yonne, to this meeting, and forthwith you propose to exploit him."

Tsubandi sat perplexed, a defensive, slightly irritated look on his face. "I told you it wasn't good!" he exploded, and his anger, which made the verdict unanimous, caused everyone to burst out laughing. Luannah who had remained silent since opening the subject, spoke up in an indulgent, conciliatory tone.

"You are all too hard on poor Tsubandi; he doesn't

deserve this treatment. The fact is, he has really suggested the right solution by telling us the wrong one. All we have to do now it set his proposition on its feet instead of on its head—which is the way dear Tsubandi's proposals often come—and we are saved!"

"How can we do this?" asked Knisslig.

"By doing as he says—dispense with the usual proceedings. But, instead of having Sir Yonne tell us about his people, we shall tell him about ours. In this way we shall be doing both ourselves and him a service. Sir Yonne will then be able to go out among our Vinibins and adapt himself more readily to our Vinibin customs; and in return, and in due time, he will be able to extend to us his own superior Earthly knowledge. Isn't that simple?"

"Excellent!" cried Knisslig. "How do you propose we go about it?"

"That is easy. Each of us represents a major field of Vinibin endeavor. We can tell him some things necessary to an understanding of our practices in these fields. At the close, we shall have given Sir Yonne a fairly rounded picture of the fundamentals of Vinibin life upon which he can build in the course of his own observations. What do you say?" She looked inquiringly at Yonne and then at the others.

"Just what I was trying to say!" declared Tsubandi dryly.

The plan was adopted at once. Yonne was altogether delighted with it. But, if he had any notion that his role now was to be an easy one, he was due for a rude jolting. The Chieftains were about to take him for a rough ride!

"The idea has become a reality," said Ehduaart good-humoredly. "And, now that it has been born, we can see, as Luannah tells us, how truly simple it is. But, to do this properly, we shall adjourn for the day so that each of us may prepare his statement in a manner best suited to Sir Yonne."

Yonne might have protested again, but it would have

been useless. The Chieftains were so eager to please him, and this plan of showing their reverence appealed to them immensely.

And so, what threatened to be a frustrating aftermath to a strange feast, turned out quite happily.

That afternoon, Vergia and Eroscheen prepared to set out for Syrwalee. Vergia sought out Yonne before leaving, and found him alone in one of the chambers overlooking the Cypress grove, absorbed in thoughts of the coming meeting. She knew what was troubling him, and smiled understandingly.

"Don't worry for lack of words, Yonne. The Chieftains will find a way—just as you and I did."

"If only you were there!" he moaned. "I'd feel lots easier."

Vergia laughed. "I'm not a Chieftain."

"Neither am I."

"You will be. Besides," she added, "I couldn't be there because I must now be off for Syrwalee."

"Now?"

"Yes—Eroscheen is waiting for me."

"I'll miss you."

"Even for one day?"

"Even for one minute."

She met his gaze, and there was a tender light in her eyes. They had been together so constantly, had shared so many strange little problems and episodes, so many moments of mutual anxiety, that they had grown closer together than either of them realized.

"I shall miss you too," she said extending her hand and letting him hold it long in his. He stood before her pressing it tenderly. He thought how much he loved her. She smiled, and he tried to speak her name but his voice wouldn't come. Inwardly, he was crying out for her, his whole being yearning for her. Then impulsively he drew her close, and there remained only the all-consuming sensation, the ecstasy of her lips upon his, the touch of her exquisite, girlish body in his arms. He heard his voice dimly as though it belonged to someone else. "Vergia, darling, I love you!"

She did not answer, but clung to him, her face upturned, her eyes melting into his as rapturously he kissed her again and again.

They were in love, the Man from Earth and the woman from Vinibus.

From across the lawn outside the voice of Eroscheen came with startling loudness calling Vergia to hurry. It brought them back to the present.

She gently disengaged herself. Confused, she brushed her hand across her forehead as one coming out of a trance.

Eroscheen's voice came lustily again. They went out to meet him.

"Please, see me off," she said, still flushed and bewildered.

At the edge of the ground Eroscheen was holding two spirited saddle horses. Bornabi was beside him.

"We shall barely have time to catch the Syrwalee conveyer," called out Eroscheen as they hurried across the grounds. He started to greet Yonne with the formal Vinibin bow, but his boyish exuberance quickly broke through this decorum.

"If we had your airship, Sir Yonne, we should not need these horses and the old conveyer!"

Bornabi turned to them with an amused grin. "I fear, Sir Yonne, that Eroscheen no longer lives upon Vinibus. He dwells among the clouds, sailing from planet to planet."

Yonne was still in the clouds himself. It was difficult to come down to mere conversation. His eyes turned longingly again upon Vergia as she affectionately stroked one of the horses. Then she mounted with the ease of an experienced rider.

Eroscheen went on extravagantly: "Time and distance no longer count in the air." He got astride his horse and turned laughingly to Yonne, "But via horseback, they still do!"

Vergia managed to get her steed a little to one side, and close to Yonne. She bent down and gave him her hand. "Good-bye, Yonne." He squeezed it and whispered, "Good-bye, Vergia. I love you!"

They were off at a gallop. Yonne and Bornabi watched them till they disappeared in a bend of the road. A deep sigh escaped Yonne, and Bornabi restrained a smile.

"You are lonely, Sir Yonne?"

Yonne nodded mechanically.

"You two have grown very fond of each other."

Yonne looked up into the Vinibin's wise, kindly face. "You have noticed?"

Bornabi chuckled.

"Is it all right?"

"It apparently is," he said laughing heartily now at the young man's discomfiture.

"Then you approve?"

Bornabi nodded and Yonne's heart leaped for joy. "Does it matter?" asked Bornabi with a shrug.

"Oh, yes!"

"Well, if you think so Sir Yonne," he replied as though humoring the Man from Earth, "I shall gladly approve."

Yonne clasped his hand warmly. He became ardently serious and began to expatiate on the new meaning life now held for him upon Vinibus. Bornabi listened with fatherly indulgence.

"How everything has changed . . . how different everything seems! Only a little while ago, I was uncertain . . . I did not know what to make of things . . . " Then, confessing in a confidential tone: "Honestly, I feared going to the

Eternal Circle because there seemed no point in my being there. Now I am impatient to go. I want to learn everything I can about Vinibus . . . to be of service to all Vinibinkind! I really look forward to the Eternal Circles."

"Ah, yes, the Eternal Circles," said Bornabi. "Your introduction to Vinibus! The Chieftains are working on their statements for you now." He added with a happy thought: "While I join them why don't you visit the children's pilgrimage now in progress?"

"Here on the estate?"

"Yes. If you will go to the clearing beyond the cypress grove, you will meet one of the groups that just arrived. This is part of 'All Beings Day' and one of my favorite ceremonies."

Yonne was glad for something to preoccupy him.

At the grove he found a great throng of children. In the center of the gathering was a platform elevated about ten feet above the ground. On it stood a young girl not over sixteen years of age. She was addressing her juvenile audience in a clear, strong voice.

This was an occasion by and for the children themselves, so Yonne found an inconspicuous spot for himself on the ground within hearing distance. The youngsters, all about fourteen to seventeen years of age, were listening to their youthful speaker with rapt attention, oblivious to Yonne's presence.

Their leader, a tall, slender girl, seemed fully at ease in her role. Yonne was a little too far away to secure an intimate view of her face, but he could see that she was attractive. Her figure was erect, and she bore herself with pleasing feminine grace. She resembled Earthly Latin types, with dark hair, and clear, olive skin. There was a dash of emotion in her voice that gave color and sincerity to her words as she addressed the assembled children in Vinibin.

69

Not a sound nor stir came from that vast audience of boys and girls as they listened to what she had to say. She seemed to hold a magnetic sway over them. Then Yonne heard these words:

"Dear friends, I might perhaps be proud to have been chosen by you as the one best able to give expression to sentiments which we share in common. But pride has no place on this present occasion; rather, a feeling of deep and abiding humility, a sense of shame and remorse. It is in a spirit of penitence that I take my part."

There was a hushed silence as she paused. What were these sorrowful thoughts this lovely girl was voicing? Why such somber utterances from such young and beautiful lips? And these children; why did they hang so earnestly upon her words?

She resumed her address:

"We are assembled here today to honor our unlike kin. Though we have not yet traveled far along the path of Vinibin life—we are but upon its threshold now, this life as Vinibins, wondrous adventure that it is, and inexplicably cruel as it is good—we feel already, each of us, a yearning to fathom its hard antinomies, to harmonize the sinister and the beautiful that it fosters in ourselves. We ponder ceaselessly this dualism in our lives, in all lives to be sure, but most assuredly in those of Vinibinkind."

The girl stretched out her arms towards her listeners, and in a solemn voice uttered a kind of lament:

"Oh Vinibin, thou strangest work of all Creation,
Vinibin who art at once the noblest of all living things;
Most zealous for the peace and welfare of your kind,
Most humble in the consciousness of life's unending
    course;
Vinibin, who art all this unto thyself, and yet,

70

Who art a dreaded monster, too,
A menace to the peace and life of every unlike kin:
Is this the apotheosis of your Vinibin ideal,
The essence of your cherished Vinibin good?
That in thy noblest work should be reflected thus,
A carnival of death for unlike kin?
Shall we not ever learn to dwell at peace
With all of nature's striving host of beings,
As we have learned to dwell among ourselves?"

The speaker gazed upon her audience. Her thoughts sounded the more uncanny to Yonne as he saw the full response they seemed to command from every child. But this was only the beginning. She proceeded:

"Incessantly this nigh imponderable question haunts our minds. We ofttimes pause at play, and during moments of communion with nature. We meditate upon this riddle, and it disturbs the enduring nature of our Vinibin joys. We ask ourselves, 'What cosmic justice, yet inscrutable to our youthful minds, contains the key to this unyielding mystery?' Life feeds upon life. From the lowest to the highest extends a battlefield of mortal conflict between all species; from the lowest to the highest, until we come at last to Vinibin-kind, to answer for ourselves. And what have we to offer in extenuation of our deadliness? With unfailing certainty comes the oft repeated answer:

"Vinibin sustenance! Vinibin well-being! Vinibin happiness."

Yonne could not believe his ears. What bitter, cynical thoughts! A plea of deep compassion followed:

"We long for reconciliation of this contradiction in our concept of the good in life. It does not seem complete or willful that our Vinibin goals should be conceived and carried out in terms of pillage and destruction of all other

71

living beings; that all our unlike kin who strive as we to feel the light of life, should have but one alternative: To serve our Vinibin needs or perish!

"This cannot be the end and aim of Vinibin endeavor: That we should be a dreaded specter in the life experience of all our unlike kin; that Vinibin pleasures should be realized in harm alone to them. As once the Gylu matched its lyric note in savory taste of tender flesh upon our Vinibin palate; so countless Vinibusian species still seem but to live for Vinibin ravishment upon the unresisting tissues of their tender bodies!"

Yonne rubbed his eyes.

There followed a kind of liturgy of invocation and response. From the speaker came:

"Oh merciless and life-destroying Vinibin,
Most ravaging of all created beings,
Hear you the outcry of your countless victims,
The mute complaint of every living thing!"

From the assembled multitude came the reply:

"Our brethren in form unlike us,
We affirm this day our faith,
That fecund soil
And glorious sun
Were created alike for all beings.
Judge us not by our will to destroy,
Nor by our daily trespasses;
For strange is the law of this struggle for life—
Futile for us to escape it . . . .
Though we ponder the secret,
The course winds unending,
For you and for us, and forever and ever."

The girl replied:

72

"And now, 'Good hail!' to every mortal being.
Though driven by the law of life to kill,
We love you well, and pray this day
That we may better learn to know your ways;
And in the intimacy of our closer tie,
To love you ever more throughout the years;
And, doing so, atone in some degree
For all the mischief we have done.
In this shall be revealed our oneness, too,
And it shall make us feel the keener our remorse."

The listeners repeated the last two lines. Then the girl waved for silence:

"Fellow playmates," she said, "let us continue as always to seek communion with our unlike kin. and to hope that in the fullness of time we shall learn to understand the inner meaning of the law of life. Our elders tell us we shall see the infinite goodness that lies deeper than the struggle to survive. We want to believe. We long to feel with them that every individual is but one small part of his own species, a vital spark that flares but momentarily, and, as its light extinguishes, serves to kindle yet another; and, so, in never-ending reciprocity to perpetuate the light of life. Till then, we vow that never shall we willfully commit a harm to any living creature, but lend our aid to beast and plant in token of our Kinship with them all."

That was it. The cermony was over. Like magic the sorrowful spell was broken. A group of stalwart young Vinibins came forward to the platform. They drew a chariot bedecked with growing flowers, and into it they escorted their girlish speaker. Upon her head they placed a wreath, and amidst joyful acclaim they drew her through the wooded lanes, followed by the throng of youngsters. In all directions they now dispersed. They formed in small groups, each carrying a tool, or portion of a nesthouse or some other material to set about their task of protecting the animals and plants of the forest against the coming winter.

Yonne breathed a sigh of relief as he heard their merry voices and laughter ringing joyously through the woods. Still, the admixture of the morbid and the gladsome in this unusual gathering baffled him. He thought of Vergia, of her charming, well-balanced personality, and of Eroscheen; and he wondered if they, too, had worried about such imponderables when they were children. Vergia had alluded to the same theme upon which this young girl dwelt in her address. Did everyone condone or encourage this morose introspection in Vinibin youth? Bornabi had called the Children's Pilgrimages his favorite ceremony!

One thing was clear. If All Beings Day was a time of atonement, it was obviously not one for wrongs committed by Vinibins against each other, but rather one for wrongs of Vinibins committed against all other living forms. Of Vinibins against all Vinibus!

The words of the girl went round in his head:

"Oh merciless and life-destroying Vinibin,
Most ravishing of all created beings,
Hear you the outcry of your countless victims,
The mute complaint of every living thing!"

If this is Vinibin religion, thought Yonne, it certainly is a far cry from anything we have on Earth!

74

VI

Early at dawn the Chieftains set out for the Eternal Circle. They gathered at the four jungle paths, and each one took a different path. Yonne accompanied Bornabi.

"Why do we separate like this?" he asked when they were alone. "We are all going to the same place."

Bornabi smiled. "It has been so from the beginning. We are all going to the same place, Sir Yonne, that is true. We shall approach it from different ways. That is important." Without waiting for a reply, he asked suddenly: "How did you like the Children's Pilgrimages?"

"I don't know."

Bornabi looked disappointed.

"I am still wondering about them."

"Ah!" His face brightened. He was all attention.

"Do all Vinibins share this belief in the affinity of all forms of life?"

"Share it? Well——" He scratched his head thoughtfully. "Why, yes, indeed," he added emphatically.

"And—about Vinibins being a menace—a dreaded enemy to all 'unlike kin,' to use the words of the young speaker—is that, too, your belief?"

"It was," said Bornabi. "The spirit and purpose of the Children's Pilgrimages are as sound today as they were in the beginning, but some of the emphasis in meaning has shifted with time and progress. We are not nearly so unkind, so ruthless in our deeds toward our unlike kin as we were at one time. But the extent to which we still seemingly trespass upon their right to life impresses our young; and it is well that it does."

"I see. Then this pilgrimage is only a kind of historical pageant; you really don't——"

"Oh yes we do!" declared Bornabi. "But our children do not as yet comprehend and feel the synthesis that integrates the individual life with the life continuity of its kind, of all species, to be sure. When once they come to learn this truth they will know that it is not so important how long or short a given individual life span may be, but rather how full and joyous it is. The duration is but a moment at any length; whence each individual passes again into the life stream of all species. That this moment be one of supreme ecstasy—this is the precious objective."

"Your faith in immortality?" asked Yonne.

"Yes."

"Then you believe in a life hereafter?"

"We believe? We know."

"You know?"

"We know there is a continuing life."

"You are certain of the immortality of Vinibins?"

"Of Vinibins?" asked Bornabi in surprise.

"Yes."

He regarded Yonne quizzically. "Of Vinibins?" he asked again. Then with a smile he added, "No, not of Vinibins, of course, not of Vinibins."

"Of whom, then?" Yonne asked perplexedly, and Bornabi burst into hearty laughter at the question.

"Well, not of Vinibins . . . that would be too absurd, Sir Yonne. When we speak of immortality we refer, of course, to the entire life-process of which every organism, Vinibin or other, is and always remains a living part."

"Oh."

76

"Yes."

"Since when do you *know* this to be so?"

"Ah, we have not always known demonstrably, I mean, until a thousand years ago. Shall I tell you how we discovered the secret?"

"Please do!"

A restrained eagerness came into Bornabi's face, a wistful smile, as though he had been waiting for this opportunity.

"It was discovered and first set forth by the greatest figure in Vinibin history," he said, "at a time when Vinibins were in desperate plight. His name was 'Dilphon-Mosa.' You will never forget the glory of that name, Sir Yonne, if you choose to dwell among us, for it holds at once the story of a great leader and a great idea."

"Tell me the story—but tell it simply," said Yonne with a smile, not wishing to be caught again in the unintelligible kind of conversation that had taken place at the Chieftains' banquet. "You have a queer pupil before you, you know, one whose mind is a total blank."

"A total blank? Hm! Ah, yes. Where would you have me begin, Sir Yonne?"

"Begin anywhere—only take care how you fill in the empty spaces!"

Bornabi knit his brow. "Very well, then, with the time of Dilphon-Mosa let it be. It is as likely a starting place as any, for it marks the close of one long era of Vinibin history, and the beginning of another: The hundred years before and after him were a turning point in Vinibin affairs. They marked a change from an age of primevalism, to one of enlightenment. Strange as it may seem to you, Sir Yonne, there had existed before Dilphon-Mosa, a thousand years ago, an era of darkness. The life of Vinibins in all lands was blighted by incessant social strife and confusion. Vinibins fought and slew each other for material booty much as did the wild beasts of our ancient jungles. Hardly ever was there a time when one could say that peace reigned in every part of the globe, so unceasing was the turmoil. It had been so with Vinibins from time immemorial; it seemed destined to continue so without end."

"Now you are talking language I understand!" declared Yonne with a chuckle, but Bornabi missed the inference. "What caused all the turmoil?"

"That is hard to say, Sir Yonne. The causes have been variously explained. Certain it is that in the beginning the savage conflict between Vinibin and Vinibin was associated with genuine scarcity of the necessities of life; so that it seemed inevitable for Vinibins to be pitted against each other in a grim struggle for existence. But as the centuries passed, our ancestors progressed to a high degree along isolated paths of achievement. Scarcity of necessities was overcome, and in the wake of mechanical invention and improved transportation, nature was made to yield bountifully. Insecurity had no longer a basis in fact. But the struggle for possession of the fruits of hand and brain did not lessen. Instead, it grew more bitter. Greater productivity seemed to make for more tense and subtle conflicts. Greed and self-aggrandizement permeated all walks of life as the total wealth of Vinibins grew in volume. The successful contenders became more powerful, and they banded together against the vanquished and the weak. Their unbounded covetousness became like a chronic perversion of all the reasoning faculties. Like some strange, accursed disease which blunted the mind, it settled upon Vinibins. The very wells of knowledge became polluted with its poisonous toxin; and truth and evil were confounded; and principles of thievery and falsehood were elevated and cloaked as an ideal for the common adoration; and false prophets brazenly condoned the wickedness of things, and held full council with despoilers in high places."

Yonne grunted. The picture proved not so strange. "A most unfortunate state of affairs," he averred.

"Yes," replied Bornabi, mistaking Yonne's remark for one of surprise. "It is not my desire, Sir Yonne, to burden you with a recital of the troublesome times of antiquity. The facts are amply recorded in our historical archives, and you can peruse them at your leisure. Let us merely remember them as the setting which led Dilphon-Mosa to undertake his great historical work. He sowed the seeds from which flowered at last a new and healthy Vinibus."

Bornabi's eyes shone as he spoke the name of the famous Vinibin.

"In the darkest hour came the light. The most ghastly and destructive of wars in all history was raging throughout Vinibus. It seemed that the evil malady that had held Vinibinkind in its grip from the beginning of time was coming finally to a crisis, and that the very existence of Vinibins was hanging in the balance. The outcome could only be self-extinction or complete deliverance.

"Then something happened. While leaders of the warring camps were seeking vainly to end age-old hostilities, their efforts frustrated only by motives of self-aggrandizement and mutual distrust, there came to pass a miracle upon Vinibus."

Yonne leaned eagerly forward. "Yes . . . ?"

"Vinibins of all lands, driven by a common suffering, became suddenly articulate by a common inspiration. It was as though, by some divine intervention, the scales of false ideals fell from their eyes, and they could see the road to peace and well-being at last.

"So clear was the road that a child could have led them to it. But it had been obscured for so long! Only the horrible decimation of war, the universal agony that gripped all Vinibus and could be borne no longer, seemed to give them new vision."

Yonne grew impatient. "What was it?"

"Ah," said Bornabi shaking his head smilingly, "not so fast. First, let me tell you about him who showed us the way."

"Dilphon-Mosa?"

"Yes. He was a Vinibin of obscure origin, born of a peasant family on the island of Humshine. The island is part of a vast chain in the Sea of Kommschein, the largest body of water on Vinibus. The islands vary greatly in climate, vegetation, and natural resources. Some of them have never even to this day been explored by Vinibins. Others have been exploited from time immemorial for their rich desposits and fertile soil.

"Humshine is of this latter class. A flat and unattractive bit of country, its land is nevertheless of the richest on all Vinibus. It was owned in Dilphon-Mosa's time by a domineering people called the Zalintherits who inhabited the mainland of a nearby continent. For centuries the natives of Humshine had to pay tribute to their powerful neighbor. Despite the natural wealth of their own country, they were forced to live in poverty; for they were comparatively few in number, and no match for the vast Zalintherit hordes that oppressed them.

"From early childhood Dilphon-Mosa had watched Vinibins of Humshine toil ceaselessly, only to see the produce of their common labor loaded on great ships and carried away to foreign shores. Little of it was ever left to find its way into their own miserable homes.

"When Dilphon-Mosa was old enough to work, he too, became a part of the toiling army of Humshine. He was not of robust stature, but he possessed a mind that was as superbly keen as his body was frail. His inquiring nature caused him to ponder this injustice. It was soon evident to him that the cause was to be found in an ancient law of plunder which had become vested with a sacred halo by its beneficiaries, a jungle law evolved in those early days of Vinibin history, when individuals had to contend with each other for the necessities of life. He could see that under this law, some Vinibins had been able to accumulate large portions of Vinibusian natural wealth and the productive machines by which it was made available for Vinibin use. Through the ages, the shrewd and the aggressive had come to acquire for selfish use these vast holdings while the great mass of Vinibins had been reduced to the state of poverty he knew so well.

"This superficial phenomenon he could see, and its disastrous effect upon the common good. But he was baffled by the tenacity with which Vinibins of all ranks protected and exalted it. Vinibins suffered by it and did not complain. This was the mystery that engaged his curiosity more even than all the mischief it created."

Yonne squirmed uncomfortably. There was an uncanny familiarity in Bornabi's words. He wanted to ask questions, but the simple manner in which Bornabi was telling his historical story deterred him.

"The critical Dilphon-Mosa quickly brought trouble upon himself by his unorthodox inquiries," went on Bornabi. "He spoke up against these prevailing evils, and urged his fellow Vinibins to abandon their jungle practices. But his words fell upon deaf ears. A few listened and understood, and they bravely helped him to carry the burden of his message. A few, more timid, did not dare openly to espouse his cause, but secretly admired him and hoped for his ultimate success. But this was not enough. Vinibins were not ready for freedom.

81

"An occasion readily presented itself to the Zalentherits to silence Dilphon-Mosa. They had become involved in one of their numerous wars with a certain rival power over Vinibusian possessions which both coveted. Dilphon-Mosa and his little band decried the real purpose of the war. The Zalintherits took quick action. They branded him an enemy of Vinibins, and in a swift, punitive expedition, arrested him and his most trusted followers. After a mock trial, all were condemned to death for high treason. But the death order was not carried out for Dilphon-Mosa. Though despairing of life and resigned to his fate, he was aided to escape by the very guards who had been assigned to turn him over to the executioner. So deeply did he impress all with whom he came in contact!

"The island of Humshine is small and the chances for escape within its borders were impossible. Dilphon-Mosa's friends gave him a small sailing vessel and some provisions. In the hope of reaching one of the distant islands, he set out alone upon the high sea.

"After drifting for days, he landed upon the shores of a small tropical island, since called Dilphon's Refuge. It was far off the course of Vinibin commerce and uninhabited.

"Nearly ten years Dilphon-Mosa dwelt there, a lone recluse, living on fruits and nuts, and on such plant life as he found to be edible. But his days were not unpleasant. There was a certain compensation in being suddenly removed from the tumultuous scenes of Vinibin affairs. The task of establishing himself safely here with only his wit and his labor as resource, was an absorbing adventure."

Yonne smiled as he compared this Vinibin Robinson Crusoe with his human counterpart.

"Dilphon's Refuge," said Bornabi, "is unsurpassed in natural beauty. Densely wooded in parts, with sunbathed fields of wild flowers and grains, it was not the worst place upon which he might have been cast. Its shores are washed by the blue waters of the Kommschein ocean, and its tropical climate is tempered by the cooling breezes of the sea. Abundant food supply makes it a haven for a great variety of bird and animal life.

"Before many days had passed Dilphon-Mosa had constructed a comfortable log cabin, stocked it with provisions found on the island, and fashioned for himself tools and utensils. He quickly set about exploring the island, and became absorbed in the wild life about him. At first, the beasts of the island were frightened of him, but soon there developed a precious friendship between him and them, a silent understanding that held new meaning and gave new vigor to his being. He was no longer a stranger to them, nor were they mute or wary in his presence.

"You may have guessed, Sir Yonne, that it was here that Dilphon-Mosa became inspired with his idea of peace and freedom for Vinibins. This idea was none other than The Kinship of All Living Things."

Yonne had indeed guessed, but he was shaking himself mentally. It all seemed farfetched. Bornabi surmised as much.

"I know this idea seems far removed from Vinibin affairs," he said. "Let me try to show you how Dilphon-Mosa found the connecting secret.

"Alone, in his intimacy with the denizens of field and forest, he felt new thoughts surging through his mind. He saw a new significance in the fecundity of living things safe from the menacing hand of Vinibins. Though life and death were a constant interplay, from the greatest to the smallest, he saw over all a vigorous striving for the momentary joy of life. He beheld the seedling as it sprouted into being, and the senile organism as it dissolved back into its elements—an endless succession of life-cycles, ephemeral, momentary; a flare of light, a thrill of sex, the twilight of senescence; then, darkness again. But it was a passing darkness only, like that of a mountain tunnel connecting two sunlit valleys, each cycle mysteriously linked to all others, each life inscrutably, but certainly, bound to every other life. There was no high and no low in the essence of the eternal stream, no beginning and no end; only the ceaseless fusion, the unending flow of the unending life process."

Bornabi stopped to look at Yonne again, this time to ask a rhetorical question for which he expected no answer:

"What was this new idea that stirred Dilphon-Mosa? Were life and death in each particular organism but the double aspect of eternal being; the ecstasy of living verily an everlasting one, a new adventure with every fecund death? Yes, it was that—but it was yet another thing, a thing more pressing, so far as Vinibins were concerned."

Bornabi did not go on at once.

They walked in silence. They came to an open space in the little jungle from which could be discerned the cypress trees looming suddenly before them in all their grandeur. Bornabi exclaimed ardently:

"There you have it!"

"Have what?"

"The trees!" He pointed to them. "They revealed the secret to Dilphon-Mosa—aye, the quality and direction of Immortality."

"The trees?" asked Yonne incredulously.

"Yes, the trees. Dilphon-Mosa records them in his memoirs, and he describes to us his feelings upon first discovering them. They were hitherto unknown to Vinibins, for they grew only upon the island where he first espied them one day on his exploratory jaunts. Rising before him in awesome stateliness, far above the surrounding vegetation, they grew in a perfect circle just as these do. These are a replica of the original grove. Are they not marvelous? Are they not an inspiration to the eye?"

"They are impressive," said Yonne, and he recalled his own exalted feeling on first seeing them from the turret.

"That is how Dilphon-Mosa felt. When he set out for them he walked for hours without seeming to come any closer. Yet always he could see their pointed crests swaying high above all other things, seemingly unattainable, yet always guiding him on. He trudged through thick underbrush, across open fields and woodland streams, through wild vegetation heavy-laden with the scent of tropical growth. Often he rested under the cooling branches of the Wahla plant.

"At last he came upon them. He penetrated the interior and found that the trees grew about a circular greensward. In the center was a floor of solid rock worn smooth by centuries of rain and weather, its massive appearance indicative of great depth.

"Within the enclosure the air was quiet and cool. Only an occasional breeze rustled through the cypress branches to break the almost sepulchral stillness. Above, the cloudless sky was like a bit of blue china topping the crests of the trees, seeming to congeal over them like some material thing.

"Enchanted by the spot, Dilphon-Mosa returned to it again and again. Then, one day came the Great Idea, born of his thoughtful hours within the still shadows of the cypress grove. In one grand moment of revelation he beheld it, and with it, the hidden force that had bent and twisted Vinibin life. He discovered it at last, the underlying cause—the First Cause—that confounded and confused Vinibin thoughts and deeds."

"What was it?" asked Yonne hanging on his words.

"It was that Vinibins had come to misconceive their

fundamental place in the order of things. Dilphon-Mosa saw all of a sudden that the deepest spiritual convictions of Vinibins had lost their positive value; that Vinibins had come to regard themselves as a divinely chosen species, fashioned by some mysteriously partial Creator as lords and masters of all created things. They had come to believe themselves, in phrases of humility, to have been ordained thus to carry out His will.

"This false exaltation of the genus Vinibin had struck deep into the spiritual life of our unfortunate ancestors. So well and firmly had it become rooted in their ideas and ideals that it seemed hardly to have been a Vinibin-made concept at all, but rather a fundamental condition of all things in the Universe, like some self-revealed truth manifest to Vinibins from the beginning of time. As Dilphon-Mosa said:

> "Vinibins took for granted that all things
> Unvinibin had been created for the special
> delectation of Vinibinkind!"

"With Vinibins all things began and all things ended. Afterwards, there was nothing; nothing but an endless death. So frightening was this thought of extinction after death that the most sanguine of our ancestral 'believers' conceived the vain hope of a final Vinibin resurrection for all time—a sort of infinite extension of the Vinibin present— a glorified returning to the scenes of Vinibinkind with its special and divine prerogatives.

"Only for Vinibins was this precious salvation ordained. It was an exclusive Vinibin prerogative. Only Vinibins might anticipate its blessed and eternally happy state. As for the other living Vinibusian forms, they were not of the Divinely Elect! Not the lowly worm, nor the stately cypress, nor the wondrous Wahla, nor the treacherous Nefarl, nor the playful Kooklwucs—nor all the infinite host of 'lesser' living things.

"Thus, in their most exalted sense, did Vinibin ideals betray their thoroughly acquisitive, their arrogant quality.

"In the shelter of his cypress grove, a lone Vinibin dweller in a world teeming with multitudinous life forms, all struggling for the momentary light of life, did Dilphon-Mosa test the cherished ideals of Vinibins and find them wanting. He saw how the instinct for self-preservation had become but a lust for possession; how Vinibin spiritual life had degenerated into a medley of theological pseudo-revelations, each contending with its rival for the special gift of Vinibin salvation, each nurtured by a blatant egotism that falsely placed the species on a pedestal above all other living beings."

Yonne was lost for sure this time, and Bornabi saw it.

"It may not be fully evident to you all at once, Sir Yonne, how this perversion in spiritual values could bring confusion into temporal things, or, how the two could be so inter-woven. It was an unconscious process—that in such exalted beings as Vinibins each individual should regard himself as a bit of protoplasmic substance of highest cosmic impor-tance. The individual had come to arrogate to himself the attributes of the race. He had come to assume that, if all Vinibusian organic and quiescent forms—*all Vinibus!*— had been created as so much chattel, so much inanimate prop-erty, to be "possessed" by Vinibins for their special delecta-tion, then, surely, each member of this race of super-beings had a divine right to busy himself accumulating the planetary morsels that had been created for him.

"Such thinking, finding its roots in the deepest spiritual convictions, became the very marrow of one's bones. Spiritual prerogatives bred temporal prerogatives; a mania of acquisition and greed, such as I have referred to, spread over the length and breadth of Vinibus. Divine providence stood on the side of the strongest, the shrewdest, the most cunning.

"Dilphon-Mosa understood this, and he knew that only a great reformation in Vinibin ethical and religious values could put an end to these predatory Vinibin mores and institutions. How to accomplish this? Whence should come the protagonists of this great cause? From those steeped beyond redemption in acquisitive practices? From their intellectual satellites and vassals who had learned to do their bidding for material rewards that might be offered?

"This did not seem likely. Then, would the protagonists have to come from those least tainted? From the great masses of the expropriated? From those same lowly Vinibins whose temporal sufferings he knew so well, who yet were spared, in their material poverty, the deeper affliction of their despoilers? Would they alone understand the message that would make all Vinibins free? Would they alone understand, as he did now, the unity of the highest and the lowliest, and discover with him the reciprocity of all life cycles, the oneness of Vinibins with unlike organic and inorganic forms? Would they alone become imbued, even as he, with a sense of the all-embracing kinship; and would it make them resplendent in its kindly ideal, revealing to them, at once, their humble role in the complete order of things, and also their true greatness; their infinitesimally small stature in the vast arena of vital transmigrations; and their glory, too, as living beings, playing a part in the eternal life process of the whole?

"With the rare vision of genius, Dilphon-Mosa foresaw that this too could not be so. For were not the dispossessed as deeply afflicted by the mania for acquisition as were the possessed? Failure in the pursuit of material holdings was no vindication.

"Dilphon-Mosa knew that in the spiritual concept of The Kinship of All Living Things sprang a well from which would flow enduring happiness for all Vinibins. It would open to them new vistas of truth far transcending the petty concerns of property. He knew that the larger Vinibin self, recognizing its oneness with the life forms of all unlike things would see that every deed committed against them *would become an act against itself.*

"It followed then, in the reciprocity of life, that every Vinibin became an attribute of the eternal life process, kin of his kin in unlike form from whom he came and to whom he would again return in the spinning of the glorious wheel of life. In the experience of universal kindliness towards the least would be engendered, most assuredly, a love of one's own closest brethren in their present Vinibin bodily state.

"Here was a spiritual concept of Vinibin stature as lofty as the dome above the cypress trees, as lowly as the creeping things beneath the rock at its base. Here was a concept of Immortality that shone alike upon all Vinibus, that knew not of the arrogance of false theological creeds, nor of prerogatives, nor of damnation. Here was a concept that kindled the spark of universal kindliness and the joy of living again and again without end!"

*   *   *   *   *

Bornabi had uttered his last words in an inspired tone. He was as one transfixed, living again through the first throes of these ethical discoveries. He looked at Yonne as from a distance. Did he understand? Was all this beyond his Earthly horizon? Bornabi wasn't sure.

All Yonne could do was express his incredulity. "I don't see," he said, "how Vinibins could have been aroused by so abstract a philosophy to abandon their evil practices."

"Ah!" exclaimed Bornabi, "I see, you anticipate my story. You are right, Sir Yonne. They did not understand. The mind could not comprehend, then, what the laboratory had not yet confirmed. And it was fortunate that this was so, for when Dilphon-Mosa returned to his native country, after an absence of ten years, Vinibins thought he had become a mystic; his enemies now considered him harmless, and they did not press the old charges against him. Though great throngs came to listen, few believed and many came only to ridicule. But the underlying truth was out and its impact upon the hearts of Vinibins struck deep. Though the conscious mind needed time to receive it, Vinibins began to talk about it and to measure their false ideals and aspirations against it.

"A hundred years had passed. Dilphon-Mosa was long dead before the great spiritual transformation, conceived after the dictates of his sound analysis, came at last into full fruition. Then, and only then did Vinibins come to understand the deeper meaning of their emancipation: The truth of the immortality of the life experience; the process of eternal rebirth in the Kinship of All Living Things."

VII

They arrived at the cypress grove. Yonne looked about.

"You have carried out the plan faithfully," he said.

"Yes. There are four such temples upon Vinibus at which gatherings similar to ours will take place."

"And what has become of the original grove?"

"That," replied Bornabi, "stands today as when Dilphon-

Mosa first saw it. The island has been preserved in its original wild state in honor of his memory. It remains a natural shrine to which each year one group of Chieftains journeys for a meeting of the Eternal Circle. During the time of their seclusion upon Dilphon's Refuge these Chieftains are as completely shut off from the rest of the inhabited globe as was Dilphon-Mosa himself when he was cast upon its shores."

"You are staunch adherents of tradition," observed Yonne.

"Yes—if tradition is vital to present well-being."

"Otherwise?"

"Otherwise," said Bornabi with a smile, "we relegate the past to the past."

They penetrated the wooded circumference where the other Chieftains were already awaiting them. There within the circle of trees was the greensward and the great rock at the center. They squatted upon the grass beside the rock as Dilphon-Mosa would have done; and the much heralded meeting of the Eternal Circle was called to order. Ehduaart addressed the group:

"Fellow Vinibins and you, Sir Yonne, our honored guest, we are now assembled in the shadows of the Eternal Circle to consider the state of Vinibin well-being. It is our desire, as it has been the desire of our predecessors at these gatherings, to help perpetuate the joy of life and humility of thought first kindled by our greatest teacher, Dilphon-Mosa. May we recommend such measures at this gathering as will serve to further the glorious ideals for which he stood.

"In the course of a thousand years, Vinibins have come to look to these annual meetings for guidance in their common undertakings. We do not want to fail them in the performance of our task. And, we must reiterate today what has been said so many times before; that our recommendations will have value only if they can stand the scrutiny of the many local agencies of Quiloth province that will test their feasibility. The fact that they emanate from the beloved cypress grove does not give them any sacred halo. We Chieftains would rather be completely rejected by an unduly critical community reaction, than be too readily accepted by an unthinking one. Our loyalty to the ideals of Dilphon-Mosa must never be reduced to a mere fetish."

A murmur of assent came from the group. Bornabi smiled at Yonne as if to say, "I hope my little story is helping you follow him."

Ehduaart continued:

"We may rejoice again this year that the self-governing provinces from which we come are blessed with general well-being. Seldom in history has there been greater cause for continued faith in the soundness of our prosperity, and for gratitude in the existing good will between the Vinibins of all lands. Since the dawn of modern enlightenment there has been an expanding joy in life for all peoples. Throughout the centuries not one drop of blood has been shed between them. There prevails a spirit of mutual help, a spirit that has been cemented into a lasting reality by the nobility of the ideals that nourish it. Such is the happy state of Vinibin affairs."

Yonne perked his human ears. It sounded like Utopia—but he kept his skepticism to himself. Ehduaart proceeded:

"Today it would be our task normally to evaluate the factors of Vinibin social practice, and to make recommendations. But, as if by the logic of some higher design, an event has occurred that overshadows even the lofty purposes of the Eternal Circle. I refer, of course, to the marvelous adventure of our distinguished Earthly visitor, Sir Yonne."

He accorded Yonne the sweeping Vinibin bow.

"The arrival of Sir Yonne has for the first time given the Eternal Circle its true cosmic proportions."

Turning to Yonne again, he said, "Our task on this occasion will be a pleasurable one. We hope it will be one for you too. We are, of course, not unmindful of our paradoxical position here as your teachers."

A ripple of laughter came from the group.

Luannah interrupted:

"Not his teachers, Ehduaart—just Vinibin commentators."

"Good," said Ehduaart; and he spoke again to Yonne.

"We shall try to place before you, Sir Yonne, the basic facts of our communal relationships. We shall try to do this in as objective a fashion as the limitations of our Vinibin understanding permit.

"These relationships, as compared to your worldly standards, will disclose to you, no doubt, many inadequacies and distortions. Ideals and practices that we hold dear will, perhaps, in your superior human judgment be seen as inimical to the common welfare. Others, appearing to us as evil, you will find endowed with the power of good. In a very real sense, you alone, Sir Yonne, will be the truly objective commentator of Vinibin life and thought. We await with eager suspense your judgment of us!"

Yonne was quite overcome by all this homage. But he fell into the spirit of the occasion, and, unconsciously, he returned the Vinibin bow to the Chieftains as a token of his appreciation. Ehduaart continued:

"In trying to decide upon the manner of presentation, we thought we could make ourselves most intelligible to you by considering Vinibin affairs in the order of their apparent cause and effect relationship: Education, Production, Ethics, Recreation, and Aesthetics. Within the time limit of our sessions, we have decided to devote one sitting to each of the first three subjects, and to combine a consideration of Recreation and Aesthetics on the fourth. We shall tell you of the last two together, not because we regard either of them as of minor importance, but rather because they are quite inseparable in our thinking.

"Before turning over the proceedings to Tsubandi who will start by telling you about Vinibin Education, I should say a word in passing about each of the chosen subjects.

"We Vinibins view our personal and collective life with Education at the base. We see the intelligent faculties not only as the fountain of all coordinated social activity, but as the starting point of the individual's understanding of his position in the whole social structure. And so, we place Education first, even before Production. Without the factor of social intelligence, production could quite conceivably lapse back into the primitive thing it once was; the shrewd, acquisitive business of self-aggrandizement which Vinibins once thought to be production." Ehduaart laughingly brushed the subject away. "That is a subject that belongs to Vinibin antiquity, and I shall not burden you with it.

"By Production as we understand it today, we mean those services and labors of Vinibinkind that are directed toward a twofold purpose: First, toward the fabrication and distribution of primary necessities; and second, toward the common expression and appreciation of the recreational and aesthetic needs of life. This is its double role.

"Production for primary necessities, in so far as it relates to food, clothing, shelter, and health, has come to be a relatively simple and mechanized function. But the whole field of Production when viewed in its widest scope, including both primary and aesthetic services, becomes a very complicated affair, and we may find it difficult to know just where its boundaries are. It partakes, indeed, of all the major aspects of Vinibin activity.

"In recent times we have become inclined to think too carelessly of primary production. We forget that it was once

94

the Nemesis of Vinibinkind, the cause of their most bitter trials and tribulations. We are apt to become lethargic with respect to it, because the vast machine has run smoothly for so long a time, and is now doing its work so well. We do forget too readily that while this phase of communal life has become an almost perfunctory one in modern terms, it was not always so."

Yonne perked his human ears. "Production a perfunctory thing?" This was hardly an orthodox Earthly proposition! He leaned forward intently.

"Not so easy a task," went on Ehduaart, "as either a review of Production or Education will be the assignment that falls to Luannah. She will probe for you our Ethical concepts, and will try to explain how these play their part in collective and private life. I doubt if it will be possible for her to demonstrate to you with full clarity, now, how intimately her field is related to Production and Education, or what strange ethical implications often lurk behind the seemingly simple mechanics of Production and Education. There is, indeed, an old Vinibin saying which runs: 'While Ethics creates nothing. Ethics molds everything.' And this is very true if rightly understood. Though Ethics reaches into every recess of Vinibin conduct, its impulse and coloration are not original with itself. It may condition a myriad of forces in all fields of Vinibin endeavor; still, the very concepts it brings to bear upon them are not the product of moral considerations but of practical necessity.

"This deep contradiction is one of the mysteries in practices upon Vinibus which we do not expect you to understand all at once. I call your attention to it at the outset so that you can guard against its confusing effect.

"When we come to the last day, Sir Yonne, Knisslig will tell you something of our recuperative and relaxational diversions—the realm of Recreation. Following him, Bornabi will touch upon the end and aim of all Vinibin endeavor: Aesthetics, the appreciation of the beautiful, the adoration of the noblest gifts of life. And that brings me to my closing comment.

"Having made some purely arbitrary verbal divisions of Vinibin social practice into Education, Production, Ethics, Recreation and Aesthetics, I want to caution you against assuming that these divisions have the independent existence implied by the arbitrary manner of words. I should point out their integration, especially with reference to their common and highest objective: The glorification of the Vinibin person. They are but the multiple exterior of an inner unity, a single complex phenomenon, carefully nurtured and guided—the full stream of Vinibin communal and private life. The purely ideational splitting up of this phenomenon in the manner in which we are doing it now is only to enable us—and for the moment you, Sir Yonne—to understand sufficiently the dynamic forces at work, the a priori conditions of present-day Vinibin life. As we Vinibins say: 'What once was not, is of the essence of that which is.' In this is disclosed to us something of the wondrous process of becoming and of being, to the end that we may direct reality in its social aspects as we will.

"An appreciation of this paradox in reality, of its continual flow through the antithesis of idea and matter, is essential if we Vinibins would avoid a fate of utter confusion. Without it we should become like hapless victims in a storm; with it we possess the key to social progress. Instead of clinging blindly to the transitory particulars of the present as though they were fixed and immutable, we can fashion and direct reality, translating it into creative social action; and in doing so, transform it forever into something new, something that partakes eternally both of its previous opposite and of its present self. In consequence, what was a way of life yesterday may no longer be one tomorrow; and, what was but a breath of verbiage—a theorization, if you will—today becomes magically divested of its ethereal garment to stand suddenly before us, a corporeal bit of reality! An institution, an art, a technique, a way of life. And so the process goes forever on. No sooner has the idea blossomed into a thing incarnate, than it is tried and judged for its claim to permanence by the same ideational striving to become of which it was once but a vaporous part!"

Ehduaart paused before driving home his point.

"Such is the fascinating dualism of reality upon Vinibus; and I presume, Sir Yonne, so it is upon Earth. In the tenacity of every tradition and in the urge for every change, there is always one supreme question that decides our course: 'What will be its effect upon the Individual?' Will it serve to unfold a full, harmonious life experience for every Vinibin? Will it leave him unfettered, unregimented? No institution is sacred, no practice tenable, no theory acceptable, unless it furthers this one grand objective."

*   *   *   *   *

With these words Ehduaart concluded his introduction to the proceedings. He sat down and looked questioningly at Yonne who was thinking hard. Yonne had nothing to say. Ehduaart turned to the Chieftains:

"I now turn over the deliberation to Tsubandi, beloved by fellow Vinibins for his services in education and shoe-making."

Yonne sat upright.

"In what?" he gasped with a start as though he had been given a physical jolt.

Ehduaart repeated obligingly. "In education and in shoe-making."

97

Yonne gulped and swallowed in silence.

Tsubandi arose. Speaking in a slow, deep voice, he went directly into his subject.

"In approaching my task, Sir Yonne, I have tried to place myself in your unique position. Coming to us from another planet, as vastly removed, no doubt, in history as in space, you are completely unfamiliar with life upon Vinibus. You are a stranger to the very elements of our social and individual existence, to all our traditions, to our past and to our present. No matter how simply I shall try to tell you about us, how can I ask you to assimilate the facts of an entire civilization? How can I do this without forcing you to take on the prejudices of first impressions gained from my remarks? Anything that I may say, to be intelligible to you, must of necessity presuppose, on your part, some knowledge of our historical setting; and of this you are wholly unfamiliar. At whatever point I shall try to begin, there is implied some knowledge of what went before—and after; and this you do not have! Do you see the difficulty? How can I recount to you any details without their context, or portray to you the historical setting without its particulars? Do you understand?"

Yonne understood only too well. His mundane ghost was forever casting its shadows across his path!

"Do the best you can," he said. "I'll try to follow."

"Thank you. I shall explain to you briefly what our basic concepts are in education, and how this field is related to others. After you have gone out among our Vinibins you will then be able to make your own observations. I hope what we tell you here will help you."

"I'm eager to hear what you have to say."

Making the inevitable Vinibin bow, Tsubandi began:

"As the handle must fit the tool, so education must fit the role the individual is destined to play in youth and in

98

adult life. What this role is to be, how effectively and fully it is to be played, this is the task of education.

"To lead forth from each individual those latent powers peculiar to himself, by which he is to achieve his useful and happy status in society calls for a twofold developmental process. Stated in terms of its practical objective, it must prepare the individual for his dual productive role, and his similarly dual aesthetic experience. Indeed, in the full expression of this aim lies the very will to live.

"This double purpose of education proceeds from the psycho-physical nature of the Vinibin being. To be wholly successful, the education of the individual must effect a full and balanced expression of his *physically productive* and his *spiritually productive* potentials.

"This observation may, perhaps, be a trite one to you, Sir Yonne. I allude to it because the fundamental need for the individual's multiple vocational expression was not always recognized by Vinibins. Not until the time of the Great Awakening in the days of Dilphon-Mosa was it understood.

"Before Dilphon-Mosa, Vinibins were educated—if we may, indeed, dignify the crude process by that term—for a single, isolated proficiency into which they 'entered' at an arbitrary stage in life. Fettered and frustrated by a host of evils inherent in their primitive economic and social institutions, and confounded by an upside-down educational system, they entered upon their productive tasks in life like animated machines. Mechanically, monotonously, they ground themselves away in some single selected vocational groove until the ravages of time and age wore them out. Then they were cast aside much as one might cast aside an old useless tool. And, the precious, multiple potentialities of the Vinibin personality became atrophied from long disuse.

"Today we have travelled far from that strange process of 'personality repression' as we now call the blind educational practices of our unfortunate ancestors."

There were nods of approval from the Chieftains.

Tsubandi proceeded.

"I am glad that Ehduaart spoke of the impossibility of segregating any given field of endeavor from all others. I have need of that thought now. Our educational life is inseparable from that of other Vinibin activities; it is, in fact, closely integrated with them. There is, for example, no given stage in the individual's development at which we can say that Education ends and Production begins. While the first is intended to prepare for the latter, still, the productive life of the child and of the youth begins long before the educational findings are complete; and the recreational and aesthetic pursuits quickly become an integral part of both.

"I shall have occasion presently to point this out to you. Meanwhile, remember one important thing: Every Vinibin is educated for a double and complementary set of vocational functions in order that he may give full expression to his psycho-physical personality. So equipped, he can become satisfyingly effective in both physical and mental productive service.

"Individual preparation for this twofold productive role involves a most complicated administrative and pedagogical technique: continuous vigilance over developmental trends; individualization of method; recording and evaluating of desires and aptitudes (which occasionally are in conflict with each other) ; integration at every point of the educational progress of the person with his productive, aesthetic, and recreational potentials and inclinations; an understanding of the total Vinibin personality.

"It would be absurd, as you humans must know far

100

beyond our meager knowledge, to assume as did our fore-fathers of antiquity that education can proceed in an institutionalized fashion, or solely along intellectualized paths, as though it were an end in itself; or that it can be made to serve as training for some single vocational outlet, either mental or physical, as though Vinibins were all mind or all matter!

"Today we no longer have any division between, let us say, manual or mental production. We realize that each individual possesses within his psycho-physical faculties both capacities, and that these must be afforded full and equal productive release if serious personality derangement is to be avoided.

"Upon Vinibus, therefore, every person is trained for and consequently performs a number of spiritual and physical productive services. He may be, among other things, a maker of clothes and a singer, as is Bornabi's charming daughter; or, a statistician, a recreational leader and a stone-mason, as is Knisslig, or a musician, a ballet dancer and a farmer, as Ehduaart; or a shoemaker and a pedagogue as myself; or he may be a producer in any other set of complementary fields which, in the course of his educational development is found to express most effectively the psycho-physical urge within him.

"Now, lest you grow confused by my apparent wanderings from education into the field of production, I shall confine myself more strictly. What you will want to know from me specifically, is this: What are the precise educational processes and techniques that we follow to effect a progressive integration of the child into the youth, the youth into the adult, and the three into one harmonious, expanding life experience.

"The ground upon which we build is the play world, that all-absorbing preoccupation of child-life through the enchanted medium of which every child endows its activities with an elixir of pure pleasure.

"In play we find genetically all the interests of youth and of adult life. It is at once imitative and suggestive of the adult pursuits. It differs from them only in that it is not burdened by the element of responsibility—though it is none the less absorbing and exciting for want of it! With a sense of pure romance, the child pursues his play objectives, sailing the high seas in a tub, building great houses of paper, harvesting the ripened grain, riding wild horses on a log; in short, conducting without inhibition, all the productive ventures of adult endeavor.

"The ever widening experience of these vicarious adventures becomes the first subject of exploitation for the pedagogue. Upon its fertile soil he builds the educational structure of the child. He fashions it to the exclusion, however, of all ethical and impersonal considerations. He proceeds only gradually to a synthesis of the purely personal with the larger social environment.

"In this entire approach is reflected the extent to which we have departed from the methods of antiquity. I must allude to them once again, to illustrate my meaning. A typical list of the 'studies' of primary and aesthetic education in the old days will astound you, Sir Yonne. Here are some of the major topics of education to which the child and the youth were prematurely exposed:

"*Geography*: The study of all the configurations of the planet, and of geological phenomena—this, at a stage when the child had not yet even had the opportunity of observing them with his own eyes, still less of comprehending them!

"*History*: A review of the entire story of the Vinibin adult world from the beginning of recorded time to the present—this, when the child was still deeply engrossed in the external phenomena of his own limited child-world.

102

"*Economics*: The study of the laws affecting the production and distribution of social wealth, though the child knew not yet how to manipulate effectively even the basic tools, and had never produced an ounce of anything.

"*Civics*: The study of formal communal organization, the subtlest of all the social sciences!

"*Literature*: The fictional interpretation and portrayal of every imaginable experience in the whole gamut of life!

"It is amazing, Sir Yonne, that these subjects, and others of like sophistication, should once have been the first objectives of education. It may sound incredible to you, but it is true. Why the child or the youth should ever have been expected to evidence either interest in or appreciation of them, it is difficult for us to understand today. It would have been no more absurd to have expected the infant to drink before it could suck, to sing before it could talk, or to dance before it could walk.

"First and last things in education have long since found their proper place upon Vinibus. Permit me, Sir Yonne, to take you hurriedly through the most important stages of the process. They break themselves into three periods, corresponding to the major developmental stages of the individual himself.

"The first, or the childhood period, extends generally into the twelfth or fourteenth years. During this stage, education confines itself exclusively, as I have already intimated, to the perspective and the consequent interests of childhood. It is concerned with a promotion of the elementary psycho-physical well-being of the child. This is attained through a development of motor-coordination, through the teaching of personal hygiene, and through the stimulation of simple mental processes. The media are formal gymnastics, games of physical exertion, swimming, walking, travelling, extended observation of and association with Vinibins and things; and, above all, through daily communion with Nature. The technique is wholly uninstitutional; the experience observational, personal and active.

"To facilitate mental growth and the sharing of these experiences we do introduce the child at an early stage to the art of reading and writing, and to the elements of mathematics. There is also commenced a simple descriptive study of some of the natural and biological sciences. Sessions on these are held out of doors, and are directly related to observation and travel. The formal teaching of them is brief and rudimentary; further development is indirect and self-taught; it proceeds as a natural and necessary means employed only in the sharing of childhood experiences. Books are hardly an item of childhood education, as you may well know from human experience."

Yonne smiled inwardly, but said nothing. Tsubandi continued:

"However, these activities form only one part of the education of the child. There is another equally important one. It relates to certain Vinibin desires that are basic, self-assertive, and demand expression very quickly. From the beginning, every Vinibin child evidences its own aesthetic and creative desires; these are, as it were, the tiny shoots from which must blossom eventually the full-grown flower. They offer a first glimpse of the aptitudes for color, sound, dimension, proportion, movement, etc., that are peculiar to every individual. They point the direction of the later vocational pursuits. To facilitate their release, children are taught to indulge freely in simple, creative arts, and in handicrafts. At first the efforts are of a purely groping nature, and wholly unproductive; but not for long. Soon the child begins to display certain proficiencies and inclinations. These are carefully watched, recorded, guided, evaluated. Potentialities begin to take tangible form; there emerges definite

104

performance in music, mechanics, painting, gymnastics, designing, horticulture, etc. The embryonic forms of the truly productive services begin to take shape.

"Creative and aesthetic development must proceed, however, hand in hand with the ever-expanding physical environment of the child-world. From the synthesis of the two opens a path of absorbing adventure. Children embark on exploratory journeys; first on small, then on greater ones. They go alone and in groups. The circle of the observable world is gradually enlarged until it has encompassed the entire globe, giving to the child both visual and mental perspective.

"A complete circuit of first childhood impressions and responses having been made, the initial stage of educational training comes to a close. The threshold of youth has been reached. The child is ready and eager for new things. He has been made conscious of his own psycho-physical potentialities; acquired a love for the great out-of-doors, and for his kin in both Vinibin and unlike form. He has experienced the first inclinations towards certain aesthetic, physical and creative values. But his habitat is still a personal and particularistic one, his experience animalistic, nonethical. He has felt the thrill of first contacts, the stimulation of first acquaintanceships; he has sensed the breadth and magnitude of his Vinibin existence. Over a period of some ten years he has traversed the far corners of the planet, and has enjoyed the pleasures of expanding motor activity. He has surveyed the globe, but he has not pondered it. The wonders of the natural and of the social world are still made of simple childish stuff; they are still one-dimensional—the present. There has been no attempt to integrate or to evaluate. The inner unity of things past and present is yet a closed secret. The child-world is but one of seeing and doing in the present.

"Up to this point, Sir Yonne, the task of education has been one of building strong the body of the young animal, and of opening wide the portals of the spirit."

Tsubandi paused, an indecisive expression on his face, as though he were debating with himself whether to dwell at greater length upon this aspect of the subject, or to go on. Something in Yonne's manner seemed to satisfy him. He decided to go on.

"We come now, Sir Yonne, to the second stage: the education of youth. The formal transition is a fascinating one, for it marks the pupil's introduction to genuine productive activity. Pure play becomes alloyed with the element of service. The child enters for the first time the wondrous halls of production. Not that there follows a life of adult responsibility. Far from it! What actually happens is that the individual becomes initiated into his role as a member of the 'Youth Community.' Here the fledgling tries his wings. Proficiencies begin to be tested and evaluated under conditions approximating adult society. I am sure, Sir Yonne, you will find nothing more exciting upon all Vinibus than the activities within these youth communities. They will disclose to you all the productive enterprises—both primary and aesthetic—of adult concern. Self-governing, still under the supervision of the educational departments, the youth communities have their own manufactories in which are produced not only the necessities of life, but also the tools, machines, houses and equipment with which youth works; they create their own music, theater, games. The youth community is the great laboratory of productive service in which the young Vinibin seeks to find himself."

Tsubandi was about to go blissfully on, but it was high time for Yonne to call a halt. His bewilderment was great and he had to unburden himself of part of it.

"Am I to understand, Tsubandi, that Vinibin education

106

is designed just to make a good producer of the individual?"

Tsubandi cocked his ear and smiled.

"You seem to have no place for culture," said Yonne, "in your scheme of education. Is culture not a consideration?"

Tsubandi remained in thought. "Hm . . . I see," he said. "You are anticipating. Yes, everything I have said so far does point to production, Sir Yonne. That is correct. And, fundamentally, production *is* culture. It is the starting point. But it is not all. I have not yet said all, Sir Yonne." Tsubandi regarded him with a kindly eye. "Production is the first consideration, culture the last. I think you will see this before I have done."

Yonne started to apologize for interrupting.

"Oh, do not apologize," protested Tsubandi. "Your question is quite in order. And lest you misunderstand, I want to say again that all activity in the youth period is still of an educational nature and purpose; nor is the transition to this period an abrupt one. Productivity, though remarkable in volume, is yet incidental. There are no quotas, no fixed requirements; there is no pace, no established technique. What is distinctive, however, is the latitude permitted to each student for making many and varied adjustments and readjustments. Early and pronounced inclinations sometimes recede; latent ones develop. First loves are abandoned for new ones. Recording and evaluating become more complicated. For each young Vinibin the motto becomes, 'Know Thyself.'

"In recent centuries, Sir Yonne, the record of youth education is indeed a gratifying one. Despite an occasional need for a re-evaluation of aptitudes and vocational goals, few instances present themselves in adult life in which the individual has not found his true stride. Added to this accomplishment, we cannot overlook the fine productive

107

work that is done by the youth communities themselves in both the primary and aesthetic services. The fact is, they are more than self-sufficient. In physical produce alone, they manufacture considerably in excess of their own requirements, and they take great pride in their annual contribution to the aggregate social wealth.

"Words fail altogether to give an adequate picture of their experimental achievements in aesthetic production. You must see them, Sir Yonne, to appreciate them. You must see their creative works in art, music, mechanics, dancing, painting; and you must have shared the enthusiasm of our young as a member of one of the youth communities, to enjoy fully the freshness and the thought-provoking originality of their ventures."

Tsubandi's face lit up in retrospect, and Yonne saw all the others were smiling reminiscently at his words.

"Creative effort," continued Tsubandi, "now begins to require the aid of comparative and historical analysis as the youth approaches adult years. The classroom rises in importance—but not yet along the cultural lines suggested by the curriculum of antiquity. Its purpose is still utilitarian, the outgrowth of a deepening interest by youth in its own preoccupation. Primary and aesthetic techniques are studied and mastered. Theory and practice in production are analyzed from the simplest methods of antiquity to the most modern ones. The natural sciences and mathematics are taken up in earnest for their bearing upon the bases of vocational pursuits. Planning, directive and organizational talents are given unrestricted play. Research and experimentation come upon the horizon. Performance in the arts acquires at last the finesse of maturity.

"But Vinibin youth is not yet ready for the final transition to adult education. I should omit a vital portion of the activities of the period were I not to mention the renewal of acquaintanceships with Vinibins of distant lands. For it is the yearning to visit again the scenes of childhood that constitutes one of the glorious experiences in every Vinibin's life. The youth period is the time of the 'wanderlust,' born of a desire to relive and enlarge those early scenes of first impressions which memories of childhood now clothe in a romantic hue. Care is taken, therefore, that every young Vinibin revisits the far corners of Vinibus to fix his sights more firmly before entering the period of adult education.

"Then, somewhere between the twentieth and twenty-fifth years, the apprenticeship of youth has been served. Personal inclinations have matured into fixed and multiple proficiencies. The formal inauguration of the young Vinibin into his dual vocational position in adult society takes place. It is an event of highest meaning to him, one that he never forgets both for the joyful festivities attending it and for the recognition of full adult status that it confers upon him.

"I shall have to pass over the 'graduate' youth's new role as an adult producer, for that is to be the subject of Ehduaart's remarks. But now starts the period of adult education. The full-grown Vinibin is for the first time ready to enter upon the study of those sophisticated subjects to which I made earlier reference: History, Language, Literature, Civics, Ethics, Economics, etc. He begins a consideration of them now because *they are a review,* an interpretation of the end results of life itself. As an adult, he is ready for that consideration; it has become a reality."

Tsubandi looked at Yonne: "Is this the culture" he asked "to which you had reference in your question?"

Yonne nodded with a grin.

"Good." Tsubandi proceeded:

"Because he has now acquired the necessary wisdom, the matured individual will understand and enjoy Vinibin culture. He will delve into the great spiritual works of Vinibus, and he will not find himself, like the unhappily bewitched child of antiquity, cast forth into a turbulent sea of unexperienced cultural values, to be left to drown there spiritually before he has yet learned to live physically; or, if, indeed, he did survive the ordeal, as a few so-called 'precocious' children strangely did, to be doomed until death, to babble a wisdom he does not know.

"For the young Vinibin adult, embarking upon his full productive responsibilities in life, culture now becomes a part of his world, the final phase. And so, his adult education begins, serving to broaden his interests and to enhance his critical outlook. He will pass judgment on the things of the past and the present; and in the fullness of time, he will effect their synthesis. He will become a critic of the social organization of which he is a part, and his dual productive and cultural contribution will constitute an increment to and an evaluation of collective performance. Finally, he will help to ignite the creative spark that enables Vinibins to fashion the trends of the future. Thus will he make *his* impression upon reality. In this, and in this alone, does culture fulfill its complete function. Less than this, its full province, it becomes an abortive thing, a force more sinister than total ignorance, creating but the pain that comes from futility."

Thus Tsubandi concluded his remarks. Yonne was disappointed, for his interest had now been thoroughly aroused. It was all so different, so completely in reverse of every Earthly concept, that his mind was in a whirl.

Tsubandi sat himself comfortably on the grass, and, as though divining Yonne's thoughts, he said:

"These are the broad aspects, Sir Yonne. You will want to know more, of course. That must come with time. For the present it would be foolish for me to overburden you with greater and more detailed analysis. You must go out among our people to see for yourself."

At this point Bornabi interrupted. "Perhaps," he said, "Sir Yonne has some questions."

Yonne, becoming suddenly the center of attention, was at a loss for words. What questions should he ask? Everything was questionable in this novel Vinibin scheme of education! Uncertain and confused, he parried for a time by putting small, irrevelant questions; but so well did Tsubandi ferret out his difficulties from them that he soon had him in the thick of the fray. Before the day was over Yonne felt like a seasoned veteran on matters of Vinibin education.

Incredulously, he asked at one point: "Do Vinibin children really engage in no classroom study of subjects like history and geography?"

"Yes," replied Tsubandi.

"None at all, say, before the age of fourteen?"

"None—and very little after that, until they have gone well into the youth period of multiple vocational training. I refer, of course, to the study of the broad cultural subjects, and to the institutional forms of the classroom. Informal, individualized, and out-of-door sessions between teacher and pupil with respect to personal hygiene, the elements of the natural sciences and to biology—these, and the simple creative activities in handicraft and aesthetics, are quite enough for the child. They are the stuff of which his child-world is composed, and by which the immature personality is enabled to expand and to understand the external environment.

"A sharing of the experiences of this world, under the subtle and restraining guidance of the teacher, affords a wide avenue of mental and bodily growth. We have learned,

Sir Yonne, that to try to superimpose, in addition, the ideology of the adult world (and this is what is implicit in nearly all the subjects once taught the child) even in a most simplified form, would be stultifying to future development. Experience has shown that it does great damage to the equilibrium of the child's personality, because the mental burden of a world unexperienced is too heavy for it to bear. The ensuing fatigue and ennui have but one effect, as our ancestors learned to their great sorrow. The child-mind, repelled instinctively by an artificial body of knowledge, develops a growing aversion to it; and upon the attainment of maturity this aversion becomes a fixed idea. The consequent stunting of mental growth thus alienates the adult forever from a genuine and an abiding thirst for knowledge.

"Full-grown Vinibins, a thousand years ago, gave ample proof of this. Freed in adult life from the cultural impositions that came too early in childhood, they shied away from them for the play-world that came too late. The spiritual works of the masters became a specter of bygone childhood nightmares, an ogre that haunted them—and of whom they spoke with respect in public to propitiate him!"

This remark elicited vigorous nods from the Chieftains to signify their hearty concurrence.

"Small wonder, then," he added, "that the records of antiquity abound in lamentations that the average mental age of adults was little more than twelve years. The ancient adult was, in truth, but an atrophied child."

Yonne pondered this. He went eagerly to another question:

"Do children upon Vinibus actually travel about the whole planet?"

"Oh, yes!" declared Tsubandi. "But it is a gradual process. Direct contact with places of beauty and with different peoples, while only of a surface nature, fixes the mental

112

horizon upon a broad stage." Tsubandi smiled. With kindly facetiousness he said, "It promotes personal modesty too, because from the start the child is taught that the hub of the planet is the axis that joins the polar extremities of Vinibus about which all things rotate equally; it is not the locus where the child happens to have been born and raised!"

Resuming his critical tone, he added:

"By journeying over Vinibus our children learn to think of their habitat as embracing the entire sphere; by living close to nature they learn to know their kin as comprising all peoples and all living things. This outlook must become a kind of a second nature. And, finally, the sharing of adventures with friends made over the length and breadth of the globe offers diversified mental stimulation."

Yonne recalled how different was the circumscribed environment of human children. The idea intrigued him.

"But what about these 'Youth Communities,'" he asked. "Do you mean that young Vinibins live apart from their elders?"

"Yes and no. The Youth Communities do have their own grounds and buildings where the educational activities of our youth are carried on. This does not necessarily mean that youth dwells apart from the rest of the community. There is often a difference in the living arrangements of many of our young Vinibins. There are those youths, for example, who live as members of a parental household; there are others who, having no families, live with groups of their own kind under communal supervision."

"No families?" broke in Yonne dubiously. "What about the child's need for parental affection?"

"A good question," observed Tsubandi. "We must indeed provide for this emotional need of the child, beginning with the earliest stages of infancy, especially if there is a strong parental fixation."

113

Yonne nodded, pleased that he had made a point. But Tsubandi's next observation undid him again:

"Of course," he said, "children differ in this respect as they do in so many other ways. While there is important participation by parents in the child's development, arrangements vary greatly. Some children are raised communally yet maintain the closest ties throughout their lives with one parent or both parents. Others shed them with amazing rapidity. The details have to be worked out in each case, and much depends on the cohabitation desires of the parents."

"The cohabitation desires of the parents?" Yonne elicited a faint, "Oh?"

"Yes," said Tsubandi laughingly. "After all, the sexual relationships of adults express themselves in varied ways, as you humans must know. Some Vinibins mate for life, others for a time, and still others not at all."

"And still others," broke in Luannah jokingly, "can't make up their minds!"

"Precisely," said Tsubandi.

"But" asked Yonne, not sure of his ground and trying to appear casual, "doesn't the young person with no parents experience hardships?"

"Hardships?" Tsubandi looked perplexed.

"I mean socially . . . that is, isn't there a social stigma attached to his status?"

"Social stigma!" Tsubandi looked shocked and surprised. The others, too, regarded Yonne in a strange, quizzical manner. He realized that his earthly background was intruding itself to the confusion of himself and everyone else. He tried to effect a retreat, but the Chieftains were after him like a pack of bloodhounds. He rephrased his question cautiously.

"What I meant was—do both groups of children progress

equally well? I mean the parental and the . . . ah . . . the others?"

"Oh," said Tsubandi brightly. "Yes, there are some differences. The parental child, for instance, is at a slight disadvantage. He has more difficulty in developing his own objective reactions. Parental influence and affection tend to have an unconscious inhibiting effect, despite all effort honestly to curb them. The parental child experiences some hesitance in adapting himself freely to the expanding environment. The non-parental child has an easier time of it. He develops more spontaneously and with less conflict. There is, strangely, however, an emotional content to the family relationship for some Vinibins that is strong and qualitatively unique. The family tie satisfies a deep need in many personalities and, thus, this closely-knit unit persists. In the end educational and observational experience overcome all obstacles; both groups of young Vinibins make their full adjustment for themselves."

Yonne was more nonplused than ever. Were these Vinibins doing everything backwards or was there something wrong with human thinking? Knisslig didn't help matters any by offering some advice.

"I believe Sir Yonne will understand this better after we have told him about our ethical practices."

"Yes," said Tsubandi, adding that the social life of the child was so completely integrated with the relationship of the adult sexes as to require quite a separate and detailed consideration. "There are," he said, "so many intermediary types of connubial arrangements between the monogamous family unit on the one hand, and the mutually desired independence of both parents on the other, that you will find them a source of fascinating study. More often than not the non-family child retains intimate ties with one or both of its parents, though no family home has ever been set up. Some of the finest friendships upon Vinibus exist between parents and children of the non-family relationships. But," he added, "this takes us quite off the subject."

Yonne jerked himself with an effort back to some other questions.

"Vinibins seem to secure productive work from their young at an early age. Isn't that what I am to infer from your remarks on production in the youth period? Young Vinibins evidently go to work very early in life."

"Work?" said Tsubandi, with a blank expression.

"Yes. You teach the young how to make things for use . . . they *do* produce things, even though, as you say, that is incidental to their further education. Isn't that so?"

"You mean the Youth Production Communities?"

"Yes."

"To be sure, they produce there. In fact, they begin much earlier in the making of useful things. You will remember, Sir Yonne, I mentioned the simple handicraft and creative activities of the younger children. Yes, we begin quite early in this most important developmental step—and this most enjoyable one, too, I might add."

Yonne was thinking hard again. This most enjoyable one? Work? Hardly! The new thought found its way gropingly into his earthly mental luggage. With it his questions began to sound foolish, even to him; but he continued almost mechanically to ask.

"They really don't work, then," he found himself saying, "do they?"

"No . . . not work," replied Tsubandi, in an uncertain voice. "They grow, develop . . . they produce, create, enjoy, they. . . ."

"I know . . . but you provide well for your young . . .

there is no pressing reason why they should have to go to . . . I mean they are not compelled to?"

"Compelled? Yes they are indeed compelled, Sir Yonne. They are compelled to do all these things by the irresistible psycho-physical urge, if we take care in releasing it properly. This is the task of education." Tsubandi regarded him questioningly: "Perhaps, this is the compulsion you have reference to?"

"Perhaps," said Yonne, but he knew that it wasn't. He went on to another subject.

"You say, Vinibins engage in more than one type of productive service. Is it not difficult for every Vinibin to find himself in two vocations?" He laughed jokingly. "We humans have all we can do to find one job on Earth, to say nothing of finding two!"

This seemingly innocent observation brought forth a really startling reaction from all the group.

"What!" exclaimed Tsubandi. "Do humans have single vocations?" His voice became a mere gasp; his face turned white. Then, suddenly, he burst into uproarious laughter in which all the Chieftains joined him.

"That was a good joke on you, Tsubandi!" cried Ehduaart. "It serves you right for jumping to conclusions."

"Don't blame Tsubandi," remarked Bornabi, still chuckling. "I think we are all guilty of suspecting the same thing."

Yonne's embarrassment turned to uneasiness.

"It is . . . funny . . . isn't it?" he said in a half whisper, his face drawn, his grin painful.

Luannah came to his rescue.

"You must forgive us, Sir Yonne. We are forever interpreting your own words as though they came from a Vinibin. Your remark was almost word for word like one of the utterances made by the ancient States Attorney who prosecuted the great Dilphon-Mosa! It was uncanny. We just could not help misinterpreting."

Yonne wiped beads of perspiration from his face.

"Most absurd of us!" said Tsubandi. "Please overlook our stupidity, and forget the incident."

Poor Yonne! He stammered an apology, and decided from now on to ask his questions more guardedly. As a result they became less revealing. But something had meanwhile been happening to his mental quietude, something that he felt had been impending from the very beginning. He had arrived at that wide destination of which vague forebodings had long made him strangely aware. He had come to a point of departure from something basic in his entire Earthly past. Feelings of apprehension possessed him again.

A strong gust of wind came rustling through the hitherto quiet cypress trees. It shook the great branches with sudden violence, and caused the Chieftains to look at each other with alarm. This, fortunately, brought an end to Yonne's predicament. Bornabi stepped outside the circle and returned immediately to say that a heavy storm was blowing up from the south. Great black clouds were darkening the horizon on all sides. The Chieftains decided hurriedly to conclude the day's proceedings.

"If this continues through tomorrow, said Ehduaart with feigned calm, "we shall return with protection and covering."

Yonne saw the troubled looks of the Chieftains but he was glad for the respite. There was a limit to what he could absorb at one time! Enough had already transpired to set him pondering not only about affairs upon Vinibus, but about those he had left behind.

VIII

The storm was fast approaching as they walked briskly back to the house. Ehduaart surveyed the sky.

"I fear we are in for it," he observed, giving a meaningful glance to the others.

"Do you have severe storms on Vinibus?" asked Yonne.

"Not often," said Ehduaart, "but when they come, they sometimes rock the planet!" He laughed, but Yonne saw it was not an easy laugh.

The wind now took on near hurricane proportions. It howled and whistled through the foliage, and sent leaves and small brush flying through the air. A blanket of fast-moving clouds hid the sun and gave a yellow, metallic color to the sky. The group had no more than reached the house when the storm broke in all its fury. The rain came down in torrents.

As Yonne stood at one of the large windows, absorbed in the violent display of Vinibusian elements, he heard a gentle voice at his side. He turned and saw Luannah smiling at him and holding a sealed note.

"A message for you, Sir Yonne."

"Me?"

"It has just arrived—from Vergia."

"From Vergia?" he gasped in open delight.

Luannah's eyes twinkled. "You are glad to hear from her?"

"Yes!"

"Then everything is as it should be," she said with a

wide grin. She gave him the note and left. Excitedly he tore open the envelope and read:

Dear Yonne:

I have just returned from the festival of the "Song of Songs." I am exhausted but happy. Amidst all the excitement I had to take time to write you these lines. Today, ten thousand singers—including me!—assembled here on the yellow sands of the Syrwalee seacoast to give expression, in a great outburst of melody, to our most cherished Vinibin songs. It was a magnificent spectacle, and never before did we sing so well. We opened the ceremonies with a hymn to the Stranger, Man. Can you guess what it was? Here are the words:

> Rejoice in song, oh Vinibins!
> A herald from the Earth has come.
> Triumphantly, the truth he brings
> That Vinibus and Earth are one.
>
> Our greetings to you, Worldly guest,
> First conqueror of cosmic space;
> The trail that follows in thy quest,
> Eternity shall not efface.
>
> Oh, Kinship of all Living Things!
> In this thy consummation lies:
> That from sidereal vistas springs,
> A harbinger of heaven's ties.

It is an inspired song, Yonne, written by our most celebrated living composer. You will hear it soon enough, for it is already on everyone's lips and on every choral program.

Need I tell you that my journey has been a kind of triumphal march? Wherever I go, throngs of Vinibins

120

besiege me with a thousand questions. I am honored and feted because the whole Vinibin world knows that I have actually seen and spoken with the Visitor from Earth!

And yet, this is not why I write you. You are in my mind constantly—not because of what is happening here! I am tormented by the thought that I could not bring myself to say to you yesterday what I have been struggling to say to myself for a long time, and what I shall tell you now without wasting another word: I love you, Yonne! There—now it is out!

Why the fact that we come from different planets should have blocked me all this time from admitting it to myself I do not know. But it doesn't matter any more, because I do love you, Yonne, and I miss you every minute I am away.

Vergia.

Yonne's mind stopped. He was in the clouds, floating in a sheer transport of pleasure. She loved him!

The storm outside became non-existent. Within and without, there was but one sensation, the surge of his own inner feelings, the all-pervading image of Vergia! Now he knew they had come together, had almost simultaneously discovered their love for each other. They had crossed that vacuous gulf of the Universe as though it had never existed, Man and Woman, timeless, placeless, drawn together by the all-consuming power of love. Now he would count the minutes and the hours that kept them apart until she would come back to him and he would again have her in his arms!

* * * * *

At dawn the Chieftains were already assembled in front of the house waiting for him. The storm had not altogether subsided, but nothing could stop the third meeting of the Eternal Circle! The Chieftains were equipped with raincoats, rubber shoes and caps. On their backs they carried folding chairs and tents neatly bundled like knapsacks, and they had a complete outfit ready for Yonne.

As he came out to join them, he observed that the storm was still the subject of anxious conversation. He heard Tsubandi say, "There is one chance of rescuing them."

"Rescue whom?" he asked.

Bornabi told him: "Large areas of Vinibus have just been struck by devastating storms."

"Yes?"

"The most violent one still rages in the Kommschein sea."

"The Kommschein sea? Why, that is where the Chieftains meet!"

Bornabi nodded.

"Are they in danger?"

"We don't know—we haven't been able to reach them."

"Then why are we standing here? My plane is at your service!"

Luannah rushed up to him impulsively. "Oh, I knew you would say that, Sir Yonne!"

"Let me go at once."

Ehduaart came forward. He put his hand gently on Yonne's shoulder.

"There is nothing, Sir Yonne, nothing—just now. We are awaiting word."

"Why wait, when I can get there quickly by plane?"

"The Kommschein sea is impassable. You could never get through it."

"I'll fly over it. Don't you understand?"

"We do understand, Sir Yonne," said Knisslig. "You can fly over the storm. But we know the Kommschein sea, and

122

the fury of its typhoons. You could not get down through them to reach the island."

"I can take a chance."

"My brave young Man," broke in Ehduaart with kindly firmness, "we Vinibins must take the first chance. We have specially constructed ships to combat the storms of the Kommschein. We must try them first, and if we fail, then, we must check the location of the storm before——"

"That may be too late," protested Yonne.

Ehduaart smiled. "Our ships are fast. We shall be kept informed."

"You are sure there is no quicker way?"

"We are sure." Ehduaart's tone left no doubt. Linking his arm affectionately into Yonne's as Bornabi was wont to do, he started with him for the cypress grove, and bade the others to follow. "Come, we have a task to complete while we are waiting. If word comes for our help we shall hear the carillon ring."

"Yes," put in Tsubandi, "the Eternal Circle demands completion."

Yonne turned anxiously to Luannah. She understood. She squeezed his arm gently. "Vergia is safe," she said.

* * * * *

Insistence on the meeting at a time like this seemed like carrying things too far to Yonne. But to the Chieftains it was all-important because it was for the benefit of the Stranger Man, and nothing was apparently so important, even the lives of a half dozen Vinibin Chieftains!

At the Cypress grove, Ehduaart resumed the proceedings without fuss or delay.

"Sir Yonne," he said, "we shall now tell you about Vinibin production. Tsubandi has already explained to you that production calls for twofold services from every Vinibin.

Upon Vinibus, everyone produces for two basic needs: Primary and Aesthetic. I shall tell you only briefly about primary production, and direct most of my remarks to the aesthetic side. This seems wise because primary production is essentially of an external, mechanistic nature, the various aspects of which lend themselves quite readily to your direct personal observation. We invite you, Sir Yonne, to visit the manufactories of primary production at your leisure."

Yonne thanked Ehduaart and assured him it would be a great honor. Ehduaart went on:

"We realize on the other hand that you could not hope to understand our productive services in Aesthetics just from direct observation. They require some explanation from us here. But, first, I'll tell you quickly a few things about primary production, then in more detail about the aesthetic field.

"As Tsubandi told you yesterday, primary production provides for all the physical necessities of life, including also the physical necessities of Aesthetic production. This is significant, and I shall have occasion to elaborate on it. Now, primary production, having for its objective the common security of Vinibins, seeks a high degree of standardization of method. This it does in the interests of economy, and it is something far different from the conditions that obtain in aesthetic production. But—the collective machine that 'has run so smoothly for so long a time' would quickly run amuck were we to neglect certain basic safeguards. We must, for example, guard against overcrystallization of method, keep eternal vigilance lest too much uniformity creep into it. Many years ago, we discovered that the highest economy results only from constant receptivity to new and improved techniques—and to diversification.

"A balance between standardization and flexibility in primary production is effected in the following manner:

124

We encourage the productive autonomy of all population groups and territorial units possessing a sufficiency of resources or an easy access to them. These units or 'Socios,' as they are called, number into the thousands upon Vinibus. They have complete independence in all matters pertaining to administrative and technical production policy. A great diversity in practice results therefore for different parts of the globe. To provide a clearing center for the best of these, all Socios are federated into the four great Provinces which we told you are represented in the Eternal Circles.

"The Provinces serve in many ways to promote equal accessibility by the Socios to each other's practices. They serve many other purposes: to coordinate policy, to regulate and plan the interchange of goods and services, to work out local quotas, to integrate a full production for all Vinibus to the mutual advantage of every part."

Ehduaart paused to add parenthetically: "The Provinces have no mandatory powers over the self-governing Socios." He grinned and looked at the Chieftains. "That is where we come in, and the annual meetings of the Eternal Circle. Only here, in the highest councils of the land, can globular productive policy be laid down with full moral suasion. And it is the recommendations we make here that the Provinces seek to interpret and to carry out in cooperation with the Socios.

"The purpose of the whole autonomous and federative scheme, Sir Yonne, is to afford on the one hand, as wide a latitude for differences in technique and policy as possible and, on the other, to make all things of benefit accessible to Vinibins of all lands. This is, broadly, the plan of organization for production of primary necessities upon Vinibus.

"I come now to Aesthetic production, which revolves around the *individual* and his cultural activities. Cultural service is of a personal and group nature. It is concerned with the promotion of aesthetics, ethics, physical and spiritual recreation, art. Its 'produce' is for the person what the primary produce is for the Socio. And so, its avenue of release is through the person and his voluntary group, rather than the total community; its method is individualistic, not collective.

"Characteristic aesthetic production includes choral festivities, gymnastic meets, dramatic presentations, pageantry, dancing, competitive sports and games of skill, orchestral performances, philosophical symposiums, and a host of other Vinibin activities.

"While there is a vast difference between the quality of the aesthetic services and those of the primary field, the points of contact between them are legion. As I have said, primary services are required in countless ways for aesthetic production. There is necessary, for example, a diversity of planning and coordinating skill in every aesthetic venture. A wide range of articles and equipment is needed jointly by both fields.

"Let me illustrate this by citing just a few instances: The same paper and ink may be used either for the sheet music of the community orchestra or for the ledger of the accountant in food production; construction materials will serve for the erecting of a clothing manufactory, or for the building of an art salon; machines that produce basic linens and silks for primary productions will also make the fabrics for the costumes of the theater; the scientific skill that can plan the heating, lighting and water system of a private dwelling place can plan it for a community music conservatory.

"At every point, material requisites, skills and techniques required in the consummation of aesthetic production call upon the departments of collectivistic or primary production, and lead to a fusion of the two. You will soon have

126

occasion to learn, Sir Yonne, how nice a problem of social accounting is presented by the task of apportioning productive effort between them."

Here, Ehduaart became amused, and he exchanged a knowing smile with the other Chieftains. "How much material and Vinibin labor hours are to go for the capital and consumer goods of the primary needs of food, clothing shelter and health—how much for the capital needs of aesthetics? This is always a moot question upon Vinibus!

"Now, Sir Yonne, I must stress an important point: It is that beyond this common economic base the integration of primary and aesthetic production does not go. In the execution of its skills, aesthetic production exists as an experience quite separate from and opposed to the collectivistic method in the primary field. In almost every respect it presents an antithesis to the former. Where the primary field calls for uniformity, the aesthetic wants differentiation. Factual data give way to poetic interpretation; material construction transcends to artistic creation; regimented energy decomposes into individualistic fantasy. Thus is the crown of aesthetic experience placed high upon but also high beyond the edifice of primary production!

"This brings me to a second basic consideration which can confuse you, and, lest you be led to some false conclusions from what I have said so far, I must caution you at once: Do not assume that the qualitative difference between aesthetic and primary production extends also to the *subject* (The Vinibin) himself. Please don't get the idea that some Vinibins function only in Primary Production and some only in Aesthetic Production. *Every Vinibin is an active participant in both fields.* Tsubandi has already emphasized this in his description of the preparatory educational process for multiple vocational services. It will be well for you always to bear it in mind. Let me clarify this for you with

127

some samples of characteristic activities engaged in by all Vinibins in the course of a day. A typical schedule is as follows:

I   Production for 'Primary' needs:
    (Daily) from 5 A.M. to 9 A.M.
II Production for 'Aesthetic' needs:
    (On specified days) from 10 A.M. to 8 P.M.

"Vinibins perform daily in the first category. They choose their time and its apportionment in the second, and this is determined by the individual's aesthetic skills and consequent group affiliations. All other time is his own. That is to say, he has productive obligation for those services in both the I and II categories for which his education qualifies him. Aside from this obligation he is a free agent. A few examples of individual production schedules will further illustrate."

Ehduaart drew a slip of paper from his pocket. "I have here, a daily schedule of three hypothetical sets of activities drawn up for three equally hypothetical Vinibins. Let me read it to you:

First Vinibin:
    From 6 A.M. to 9 A.M. (Primary Production) He is engaged in the performance of certain routine operations in the manufacture of shoes.
    From 9 A.M. to 4 P.M. This is the leisure-time portion of his day during which he occupies himself as he pleases. He may join in recreational sports (aesthetic appreciation, nature communion, or in any of the social activities of the day; or he may choose to do nothing.
    From 4 P.M. to 6 P.M. (Aesthetic Production and Adult Education) He performs once in five days as a cellist in the local symphony orchestra. For other days, the period

is divided between scheduled classes in adult education, and rehearsal for orchestral appearance.

From 6 P.M. to 6 A.M. This again, is unscheduled. It is customary upon Vinibus to retire shortly after sundown. Except for certain emergency productive functions collective activity ceases at 8 P.M.

Second Vinibin:

From 6 A.M. to 10 A.M. He is engaged in production of a synthetic building material. Time is scheduled to include the duties of (1) wrapper in the shipping department; (2) chemist in the testing laboratory.

From 10 A.M. to 3 P.M. Leisure time.

From 3 P.M. to 5 P.M. He is a ballet dancer. Performs once every four days; other time is spent in further study of his chosen art.

From 5 P.M. to 6 P.M. He has daily classes in adult education.

From 6 P.M. to 6 A.M. Leisure time and retirement.

Third Vinibin:

From 5 A.M. to 9 A.M. He is engaged in agriculture as a truck farmer. Time is apportioned for two sets of duties: (1) production in the field; (2) production in the laboratory, as a research student in plant bacteriology.

From 9 A.M. to 2 P.M. Leisure time.

From 2 P.M. to 4 P.M. Performs as an actor in the community theater. Presentations are given once every ten days.

From 4 P.M. to 6 P.M. Adult education.

From 6 P.M. to 6 A.M. Leisure time and retirement.

Ehduaart looked up. He smiled at Yonne's expression of skepticism, and resumed his address in a slightly apologetic tone.

"I am aware, Sir Yonne, that this gives you but a scant idea. It is just a rough illustration of the principle on which Vinibin production and leisure time are divided for a given day. Schedules are worked out on an annual basis by all individuals in accordance with local regulations and needs, and after consultation with superiors or coordinates as the case may be. The characteristic features common to all of them are the points I have tried to explain to you. They are:

1. That every Vinibin engages in a multiplicity of productive functions.

2. That these functions are of a complementary nature (psycho-physical) for which the education of the individual has fitted him.

3. That every Vinibin continues his educational training during the entire adult productive stage.

4. That all Vinibins share equally (though not in the same manner) in productive and leisure time activities.

"Some further information that you may glean from this simple breakdown is:

1. That primary production is carried out in the early morning hours, and on a daily basis for every individual.

2. That aesthetic production calls not for daily, but for periodic service on specified days of the month and the year. A competitive sport may afford entertainment and diversion once in five days; a symphony orchestra may give its concerts once in every ten days; a choral group may sing at similar intervals; an art club, a gymnastic team, a literary group may give exhibitions on specified occasions. The countless aesthetic ventures participated in by all adults (to say nothing about those of the 'Youth Production Communities') afford much of cultural, recreational and amusement interest to fill the day. No

individual has an undue demand placed upon him for his aesthetic services; he finds himself far more often in the role of spectator than in that of performer.

3. That leisure time is set aside for those portions of the the day when all nature is in its sunlit splendor.

"There are certain exceptions to this general arrangement. At any given time a small percentage of the population must always be 'on duty' for indispensable and emergency services. These include key positions in public safety and health, in transportation, and communication.

"I should call your attention here, also, to an important deduction that we must make from the available production-time of every individual. Dependent on local conditions, from one-tenth to one-fifth of every adult's time is spent in travel. This is independent of the normal daily leisure periods. You will recall, Sir Yonne, how important a part travel plays in the life of our youth and children. Its full blessings, however, are bestowed only after the individual has reached his adult years. Then only does he derive that deep, mellow pleasure that comes of revisiting the scenes of childhood and of youth, and of renewing the many friendships made in distant lands. It would be a pity, indeed, if the diversion of travel, that most delightful and refreshing experience in life, were to be abandoned at a time when it can be most fully enjoyed.

"But to return to the productive scheme; a few more important aspects I should mention before bringing my remarks to a close. One of these concerns the matter of individual adjustment and mobility. The chosen double calling of a Vinibin is not necessarily fixed for life. There is sometimes occasion to change one part or the entire combination, either because of changing social needs, or less frequently, because of changes in the individual himself. Tsubandi has mentioned that educational training proceeds throughout all adult life. New interests, and belated talents which require vocational readjustment sometimes come to the fore in this last educational period. Experience has taught us that it is in the interests of social progress as well as individual well-being that we give full recognition to this fact. We can point to some of the finest examples of distinguished service that come from Vinibins who have found themselves late in life.

"With respect to the requirements of social mobility we are confronted by a problem of natural causes. There are times when unforeseeable developments, such as those which may grow out of climatic variations, make necessary sudden shifts in productive emphasis. Every Vinibin is ready and prepared to meet these contingencies. By training he is capable of changing to second, to third, and even to fourth vocational abilities. His education, as you already know, has qualified him for multiple services. Those which he chose in the first instance were his best proficiencies, not his only ones.

"Quite deliberately I have left for my closing remarks a word about the greatest achievement that has arisen out of dual vocational service. This is the psychological victory over the age-old evil of personal arrogance and cupidity. It has democratized Vinibin ideals as no other force has ever done.

"The principle of psycho-physical expression in productive activity has become the 'open door' to an understanding of the individual's true status in his social relationships. By virtue of its broadening influence, all things manifest themselves in their true perspective. For Vinibins, no task is too menial to be performed, no artistic expression too eclectic to have lost its social integrity. The contrasting services performed by everyone in both mental and physical vocations place all endeavor on a plane of equal esteem, and lend unflagging interest to the tasks that must be done. They broaden our knowledge and balance our viewpoints. To the modern Vinibin no field is a closed book, and no status beneath or above him. In his dual creative capacity he can say at last that the artist has become a shoemaker, and the carpenter, a poet; until the final day of Vinibin dissolution, life becomes for everyone a fascinating adventure, an adventure that will cease to be only with the commencement of new and ever changing cycles through the multitudinous life forms of our unlike kin."

Ehduaart bowed to Yonne, then sat down upon the grass. He remained silent a while, then urged, as Tsubandi had done, that Yonne question him on what he had said.

As on the previous day, Yonne's sense of the practical was still rebellious to all that he was hearing. The new ethical vistas these Vinibins were opening before his unbelieving eyes seemed more like Utopian proposals to remake the world than the factual data of a planetary civilization. He could not believe that the Vinibin plan actually worked.

In this strained mood he approached his inquiry. Some basic facts, however, had become clear. He realized that Vinibins had discarded the human concept of title to productive machinery and natural resources. The very concept of private "title" to any portion of the planet was foreign to their thinking. Nor did they seem to have anything like state ownership. Both ideas were apparently unknown to them or had been relegated to the distant past. Instead there was the all-pervading idea of the The Kinship of All Living Things which had engendered a universality of outlook, a kindliness of thought that simply precluded our petty Earthly notions of ownership either private or state.

Still, he was hardly ready to accept what he had heard. He began to draw comparisons. He felt certain from his worldly viewpoint that human beings could never function under such a lofty scheme of things. We humans, he reasoned, need the stimulus of grim economic necessity and the incentive for personal gain to spur us on. The selfish motive, whatever the cause, is paramount with us. Of that there could be no mistake. Could we ever hope to sublimate it in the manner that these Vinibins had so nobly done? Was it, indeed, a matter of sublimation, or was it . . . ?

Yonne checked his roaming thoughts. What had all this to do with affairs upon Earth? He was no longer on Earth. These good Vinibins were not concerned with ways of life upon Earth. Nor were they trying to persuade him of anything superior in their own scheme. They had, in fact, the most implicit confidence in human superiority, and were trying merely to enlighten him as to their Vinibin customs; so that he might adjust himself happily among them; perchance, in the end, that he might teach them the superior quality of human affairs.

How strange! How utterly preposterous was his role becoming!

But the impulse to judge in terms of human values would not leave him. He found himself interrogating Ehduaart more out of speculation on the applicability of Vinibin ideas to the human order, than out of a desire to learn. And in the light of Ehduaart's replies he was being driven inexorably towards a vague, distant goal. One question served rather strikingly to illustrate this. He had asked:

"How do you attain a high degree of efficiency in productive effort under your purely voluntary arrangements for the individual's services?"

"Efficiency?" asked Ehduaart. "I do not know what you mean."

He put his question another way:

"How are you assured of the individual's maximum

efforts to produce. I am thinking of the need of society to effect a maximum in output at a minimum of cost and waste. I have in mind the incentive, as we humans know it, that drives people on to produce to their utmost capacity."

Ehduaart regarded Yonne in the quizzical manner that was now becoming more frequently evident.

"I do not think," he replied at last, "that we Vinibins are interested in this thing you call "efficiency." We do not try to attain what you call a maximum—or a minimum—in anything we do, least of all in matters of production."

Yonne pursed his lips in thought as Ehduaart went on to elaborate.

"Perhaps, I should say we Vinibins do not *want* to produce the greatest possible quantity of goods, or to secure from any Vinibin a maximum of productive effort. That would be disastrous. Historically, we have good cause to believe that such a productive policy would result in quite the opposite of what we really desire. It would create in us a mania for productivity so uncontrollable as to sap us of our best strength. We should, I fear, become the slaves of production rather than its beneficiaries."

This rang a bell in Yonne's earthly past. He asked to hear more.

"Permit me then, Sir Yonne, to analyze a little further for you this objective you call maximum effort. Wherein lies its evil?

"Well, I believe you will find it to be subtly concealed in the predisposition that is fostered by any concept of maximums. For example: To approach the task of production with this aim would arouse in the mind possessive desires of an unrestrictive kind. Such desires, while in their prenatal state within the mind, might appear lofty enough; but, once translated into action, they would lead inevitably, by the law of their unbounded pretensions, to no end of trouble.

They would create in us an insatiable thirst for more and more—and more! We should, like our unfortunate ancestors, soon be afflicted with a lust for unlimited personal acquisition. Like a host of tyrannical imps, our acquisitive desires would rule our lives, exacting ever greater demands of us, luring us on with temptations of false material reward, until they would have driven us into a frenzy of greed for maximums! And in the end, we should be tricked out of our reward by a condition of chronic exhaustion that would rob us of the very will to enjoy the fruits of our labor."

The expression on Ehduaart's face became tense. There was something sharp and compelling in his voice. Then, almost bitterly, as though he knew too well whereof he spoke, he said:

"This, Sir Yonne, is the Vinibin fear of maximums in production."

His words rang in Yonne's ears like an accusation. Yonne felt a sense of guilt under his stare. There followed a strained silence. Then, as if by design, a light rustle in the cypress branches attracted their attention. Yonne turned to look. A little bird, the Daifili, was fluttering nervously to and fro in a state of great agitation. Presently he noticed that it was engaged in trying to extricate a bit of ribbon entwined in the foliage. The little fellow pulled and turned and twisted in a valiant effort to free the cloth from the tree, but to no avail. Twice the Daifili flew away as if to abandon the task. But each time it returned, flitting about with loud screeching to renew the struggle. Finally, when everyone thought it was about to give up, the Daifili surprised them by pulling the cloth loose with one grand super-tug!

Yonne was admiring the little creature's pluck. Not a word had been spoken. Ehduaart, his eyes still resting on the spot where the Daifili had labored, returned reflectively to the subject under discussion.

"I could take you back, Sir Yonne, to Vinibin antiquity and paint for you a startling picture of a society based on the concept of efficiency. But all this," he said, waving his hand as if to dismiss the subject, "would require our delving into the archives of history, and we are not gathered now for that purpose. Some day, Sir Yonne, you will want to look up this unhappy Vinibin evidence of a long forgotten past."

But Yonne was not satisfied. Something in Ehduaart's logic went straight home, hitting the core of his most cherished human ideals. He balked. He was even a little angry with Ehduaart, and his unconscious was bristling with a defensive emotional armor to ward off a strangely telling blow. He spoke with forced calm.

"What you say is interesting, Ehduaart, but I don't think it is wholly correct."

"Indeed!" replied Ehduaart with a great show of interest. "Tell me wherein I err?"

Yonne hesitated. There was a point he wanted desperately to make. It was flitting elusively through his mind. He tried to catch it.

"Now let me see . . ."

His mental chase became rapid, almost frantic. With a sense of futility, he found his thoughts beginning to wander; his precious idea was eluding him . . . fluttering away like the little Daifili with a bit of ribbon . . .

"That's it!" he cried.

Ehduaart laughed. "What?"

"The little bird . . . I have been thinking about it. I thought I saw in its struggle an answer to your Vinibin logic.

"Really?"

"Yes! You have seen how tenaciously it labored to gain its objective. Now, I presume, that bit of cloth was to serve as building material for a nest. The Daifili measured its efforts by the importance of the need. Nothing less than the

137

fullest exertion would suffice. It was determined not to give up the struggle until the ribbon had been secured. The end may at times have seemed impossible of accomplishment. But the bird would not accept defeat. It continued despite the seeming hopelessness of the task. It put forth every iota of strength that was in its little body. To use my own expression, it exerted the maximum effort. Anything short of that would have meant failure. The Daifili could not afford to set in advance any limits beyond which it would not go. Had it done so we should have seen it depart without its reward. That is a simple bit of logic, isn't it?"

"So it is." said Ehduaart smilingly.

"And is it not the same with us? Can we afford to prescribe in any manner the limits of our efforts if we are to attain the ends for which we strive? A maximum in exertion would, therefore, seem to be the price of true success. That is the thought I wanted to express when I referred to efficiency in production."

Yonne was pleased with his illustration, especially so when Ehduaart's first words were:

"You are right, Sir Yonne . . . you are right both as to the bird and as to Vinibins. But," he added, "you have not drawn the proper analogy between my remarks and the example of effort displayed by the Daifili. This is quite pardonable, to be sure, considering your unfamiliarity with Vinibin affairs."

Yonne winced, but Ehduaart seemed not to notice, and continued. "You did, however, point out your own error when you said that the bird measured its efforts by the importance of the need. Therein lies the answer to your question. Perhaps you have misdefined your term. The difference between efficiency as I understood your statement of it, and the Daifili's determination to succeed, is to be found in the nature of the objective. The bird had before

138

it a clearly limited and specific need—the building of a nest for its young. Within the confines of this well-defined objective there could be no shirking of the task. But once the work was completed, the need fulfilled—well, it would have been a foolish bird indeed to have continued to hunt madly for more ribbons just for the sake of accummulating them though it had need for but one nest! Such blind, relentless zeal to labor endlessly without regard for true need or individual well-being would have been quite another matter. Even our less rational feathered kin have the wisdom to avoid this kind of diligence. But we Vinibins have not always known it. There was a time when the purely hypothetical point you are raising, Sir Yonne, had a basis in fact in our collective life. Our conception of individual effort was ill nurtured by a desire for personal aggrandizement; our productive standards were designed not to meet a genuine need, but to pander to the lust for private possession."

Yonne retreated to safer ground.

"Who is to define the need?" he asked. "Is this not also a kind of bottomless thing, an ever changing and widening concept?"

Ehduaart raised his eyes in surprise. "Ah," he cried, "there you have touched upon a knotty problem. Over that we Vinibins lose more sleep than we like. Administratively, it is a simple enough problem to be settled in terms of social accounting and statistics. But objectively, it is not so easy. When we come to the task of evaluating the claims of every want and desire to be satisfied, we Vinibins are often sorely perplexed. There are differences of individual outlook, of group interest, which must be harmonized. Who makes the decision? No single authority or group, of course. There is indeed no single answer. The Chieftains, annually elected to the Eternal Circle, make the basic recommendations.

But, in the last analysis, each Socio decides for itself through its own administrative councils, the immediate questions of apportioning local productive effort. The more far-reaching function of interpreting the voluminous and complicated data for all Vinibus calls for great wisdom indeed, for upon the results of this are set the limits of communal productive policy."

Yonne did not press the point. There were too many other questions raised in Ehduaart's statement that stirred his imagination. He was aware that it would be futile for him to try to secure an immediate answer to all of them now. He thought again of the Vinibin production schedules:

"Do Vinbins conclude daily production for the basic necessities at 9 or 10 o'clock in the morning?"

"That is right, except for those key services considered emergent and indispensable."

"But you say these consume but a small amount of time, and affect only a small part of the population."

"Yes."

"Hm!" Yonne scratched his head. Ehduaart grinned.

"But do you find that three or four hours are sufficient in which to produce all the things required for your material needs?"

"Ample time! There is, in fact, considerable discussion at present to reduce them, and some Socios are trying an alternate day schedule as an experimental venture. Of course," he added, "this economy of effort would never have been possible before the day of multiple services for every Vinibin. Today, not only a part, but all the population contributes to material production. This has doubled and trebled the so-called available 'Vinibinpower.' Our morning services are, therefore, undergoing a steady curtailment."

"And the rest of the day? Is the individual free to indulge in cultural and recreational activity?"

140

"Well, yes—though I shouldn't put it just that way," said Ehduaart. "He participates in them in much the same responsible manner as he does in primary production. Though the conditions are not subject to the same standardization, and the services are only periodical, there is a well-ordered plan of the midday and afternoon Vinibin preoccupations."

"Of course . . . of course," said Yonne growing quite excited now. The thing still sounded like a panacea. But it began to captivate him. He recalled the earthly way, and to his surprise, he shuddered at the contrast. The image of one familiar scene arose clearly in his mind: He saw a procession of city and suburbanite dwellers trudging to work; the day-laborers, the factory-workers, the office clerks, the storekeepers the merchants; aye, the executives, all of them marching, vast gray masses of regimented human beings, marching. The sun was rising to herald the coming of day, but they saw it not. With dull, even step they kept on marching. They came at last to great stone structures about which throngs of other humans swarmed like ants, in feverish activity. Then they broke ranks and entered—like convicts sentenced to life imprisonment! Into their houses of "work" they went, to be incarcerated there behind massive walls; to toil there at close tasks under artificial light—yes, it was true!—to grind away there at some single, stultifying, humiliating vocational operation!

Great industrial establishments these were—the monuments to human achievement! Like medieval dungeons they appeared to him now in contrast to this Vinibin picture that the Chieftains were unfolding.

Deeply buried frustrations suddenly welled up in Yonne from that same reservoir of his unconscious that only a few moments ago had been his censor. He remembered how he used to feel vaguely discontented with his own lot on Earth. He remembered how he used to cast longing glances at the sun while journeying to and from his "job," and how the bonds of confinement would feel the more tortuous by the very consciousness of this frustrating experience. Especially in the spring and autumn did his fate seem unbearable! And he remembered how he was never satisfied, always thinking that the other fellow's pasture was greener, more sunlit, than his. Ah, yes! he, too, used to chafe under the frustration of a singular vocational imprisonment!

And yet, it had never occurred to him—or to human beings generally—that anything basic was wrong with things.

Unhappiness? Discontent? Repression? Yes, there was much of that; but it was all accepted axiomatically as the inevitable, bitter portion of the cup of life. The young revolted sometimes, but they were soon broken like young colts in a rodeo. They grew old in the harness.

* * * * *

Yonne's thoughts startled him! He had not yet set foot off Bornabi's estate to see things for himself, but already he was permitting himself to be carried away without the slightest verification by the glowing accounts of these Chieftains.

With his usual uncanny clairvoyance Ehduaart read Yonne's thoughts:

"What we say here, Sir Yonne, may seem strange to you who are strange in the ways of our planet. But soon you will go out amongst our Vinibins to see for yourself. Then you will judge how we apply the principles we are trying to outline for you."

"That I shall certainly do!" Yonne replied with fervor.

* * * * *

And so ended the third session of the Eternal Circle while the day was still young.

IX

Bornabi and Yonne retraced their steps along the little jungle path. The weather had cleared, and the sun was sending yellow streamers through the tropical foliage. Raindrops still clung to the leaves and twigs making them sparkle and glisten under the shafts of sunlight that pierced the shadowy spaces. Sometimes the watery prisms were burst asunder in a radial display of color to illuminate the dark jungle recesses. Sometimes wild flowers peeped forth between deep green ferns and mauve colored moss.

Bornabi was inclined to linger on the way, but Yonne's thoughts were elsewhere.

"I wonder if Vergia has come back yet?" he asked.

"Oh," replied Bornabi coming out of his reverie, "didn't I tell you?"

"No. She was to be gone only a day."

"The storm has blocked the roads from Syrwalee."

Yonne stiffened with concern.

"Don't worry. She is safe, and the road should be clear by tomorrow."

"Then she won't return today?"

"I'm afraid not."

"We haven't heard the carillon," said Yonne. "What does that mean?"

"I don't know. We are to be notified if we can be of help to the Chieftains on Humshine."

"The Chieftains may still be in danger?"

"Yes—but I hope not." Bornabi shook his head thoughtfully. "The typhoons of the Kommschein are devastating."

The thought that the Chieftains might be killed in the storm made Yonne think of the Vinibin idea of immortality.

"Vinibins should be able to view death with equanimity," he suggested.

Bornabi glanced at him vaguely.

". . . Your belief in immortality."

Bornabi knit his brow. "Immortality is more than a belief with us."

"Yes—I know."

"For more than a thousand years, Sir Yonne, we have come to understand the chemical process by which our affinity with all living things is affected."

"Then that settles it!" exclaimed Yonne with a sudden idea.

"Settles what?"

"The transmigration of souls. There is a belief on Earth that the soul transmigrates into other beings."

Bornabi looked at Yonne, then burst into laughter. "You will have your jokes, Sir Yonne!"

"But I am not joking."

"No? Well, it is not as simple as all that. We know the sequence of what occurs in the reciprocal process of dissolution and creation in all life forms, and we can see the complete integration of all things from it. Like the law of the conservation of energy, we can see that there is a law of the conservation of life. We have discovered that the myriads of individual forms—in their coming and going—manifest themselves like an efflorescent reflection of the eternal life process, but they neither add to nor detract from the totality of life."

Bornabi was still grinning like an indulgent schoolteacher. "You see, Sir Yonne, although I cannot assure you that my

144

eventual personal demise will be compensated for by, let me say, the birth of an ox, I do know from the evidence that the chemical reactions attending my bodily dissolution will bring into play an exactly balanced process of devitalization and germination."

Yonne grunted with disinterest.

"You do not understand?" said Bornabi.

"Yes—but it's no longer so exciting."

"Why do you say that?"

Yonne laughed. "I thought it would be more sensational. I mean your prospect of future life—it doesn't especially allure me."

"Doesn't allure you?" exclaimed Bornabi. "I ask you but to behold the world of life forms about us for your answer."

"I'll settle for my present form."

"My dear Sir Yonne!" said Bornabi with the slightest trace of exasperation, "you cannot be serious."

"Ah, but I am," replied Yonne enjoying this little tiff. "I am not a bit intrigued by the prospect of being turned into an assortment of . . . of . . . well, of worms, beetles, grasshoppers!"

Bornabi did not let him finish. "Aha!" he declared, his face brightening. He took Yonne's arm and, pointing to some tall, swaying blades of grass, led him to the side of the road.

"There . . . do you see them?"

"Where?"

"I'll show you!" He took a deep breath of the fresh country air and let out a sigh of contentment. "Ah, Sir Yonne, do you feel the delightful breeze blowing across the field?"

"Yes, of course," said Yonne shrugging his shoulder.

"Come, we'll leave the road and walk amidst the high grass." Bornabi's manner became eager. Then suddenly he exclaimed: "Look!—there he is." He pointed to a tall flower swaying in the sunlight on which there was perched a common grasshopper. "Careful! Sir Yonne," he whispered. "Let us approach him slowly. There . . . now . . . see him? A plain, but saucy little fellow. See how he clings with his sturdy legs to the swaying stem? Observe him well! Watch: He is setting himself for a jump. His body is poised. There! —the quick, sudden movement, the release of a tiny spring. Ah!—there he goes, sailing away in a great arc—high in the air through the summer breeze!"

Bornabi turned to Yonne with a trimphant smile. "A great leap it was, wouldn't you say so, Sir Yonne?"

"Creditable," conceded Yonne.

"Fully five hundred times the height and weight of his own little body."

"Really!"

"Did you ever jump like that through the summer air, Sir Yonne?"

Yonne laughed.

"You'll admit it has its own fascination. Come, let us go where the wild flowers and grasses grow more thickly. Here, we can drop to our knees, and explore the base of his little world."

They crawled on all fours. It was getting to be fun, and Yonne felt like a boy playing at "being wild beasts of the jungle." The high foliage rose above their heads; the sky was pierced and latticed by the stems of flowers and blades of grass. Bornabi's gaze was upon the ground.

"Here," he said, "look at this fellow scurrying to safety at our approach." Yonne saw a cricket.

"Another denizen of the smaller world, Sir Yonne. He is not aware of us. He feels securely hidden by the vast, impenetrable forest of leaves and shrubs. See how he saunters among the tiny shoots of grass. How close he lives to the warm soil of Vinibus, amidst the giant wild flowers and weeds. What sweet-scented perfumes fill the air in his small world! Observe his colorful neighbors—the busy brown and red ant, the great beetle, the downy-furred caterpillar, a nameless host of living things. What thickly inhabited jungles, these green fields at our very feet! What abundance of food—delicious morsels of fresh growing bits unknown and unknowable to the Vinibin palate!"

Bornabi paused to look up at Yonne. Then with a nod of his head and a kindly smile he said:

"No need to despise the multitudinous life-experience that meets our gaze here. At every turn it unfolds itself under the same life-giving sun as yours and mine. We get only a fragmentary glimpse of it. And these lives? They are but a momentary flare, even as yours and mine; circumscribed, incomplete; but throbbing, active, prolific, each life its own peculiar adventure while it lasts. Here, too, at our feet is the wondrous world of play, of work, of growth, of hunger, of sleep. Yes, and here too, is the ecstasy of sex, and the mysterious thrill of asexual reproduction; unique lives to be experienced forever anew with every birth."

It was now Bornabi who shrugged his shoulders. With a gesture that seemed to denote the obvious, he added: "No need to lament the brevity of our own particular existence as Vinibins—or Men. That would be like refusing the proffered cup from the fountain of youth!" He laughed, but his tone quickly became serious again.

"Another joy these tiny Vinibusian beings have that can never wholly be our own: The undiluted pleasure of the present. No faculty of memory intrudes itself to disturb the full enjoyment of contemporary things. No qualms of conscience to thwart the impulse of the moment. No fear of future, of impending death from the crushing weight of a Vinibin foot. No regrets for the past, for what might have been! No inhibitions, no doubts, no obligations! Only the fascinating, self-sufficient moments of the present.

"Where does the speculation stop? With what life forms are the sensations of life not unique? When is the call of love not rapturous, the thrill of sex not ecstatic? Who is to say: 'This is beautiful, this is not?' Upon what life forms does the sun not shine or cast its warmth? Aye, who would despise even the transitory dark and stillness of the life beneath the crust of Vinibus?

"So might we put our questions, Sir Yonne, without end or answer. Where *does* the adventure of life end, and who would judge the inner content of each stream of consciousness that flows in endless currents for the invisible amoeba as for the idealistic Vinibin?"

Bornabi observed Yonne intently. "But enough of this now," he said. "Tomorrow you shall hear more."

* * * * *

But there was to be no tomorrow—there was to be no further meeting of the Eternal Circle—not for Yonne at least. His adventure upon Bornabi's estate was suddenly to be cut short.

They had just returned to the road when there echoed through the woods the chimes of the carillon.

"Oh, oh," said Bornabi, "let us hurry."

They ran and, to Yonne's surprise, found Eroscheen waiting for them at the edge of the little jungle. All the Chieftains emerged from the winding paths about the same time.

"What's the news?" cried Bornabi.

"The last report just came in" said Eroscheen. "The storm has not yet struck Kommschein!"

Knisslig let out a happy shout. "Then the Chieftains are safe!"

"Wait!" cried Eroscheen. "They are safe—but the typhoon is fast approaching the area of the island."

148

They gathered about him, and he turned to Yonne.

"As soon as I learned of your offer, Sir Yonne, to fly to the Chieftains, I left Syrwalee. Fortunately, I got away just before the storm broke. I arrived here a few minutes ago with a number of barges carrying samples of fuel."

"Fuel?"

"For the airship, Sir Yonne."

"To be sure!" cried Yonne slapping his forehead. "And you thought of that?"

Eroscheen grinned.

"Has no one been able to reach the Chieftains?" asked Ehduaart.

"The Kommschein sea is still impassable, a thousand miles to all sides," said Eroscheen. "Not a ship has broken through, and five have been lost."

"Then, there is no time to be lost," cried Yonne.

"May I go with you, Sir Yonne?" Eroscheen eyed him half timidly, half eagerly.

"You are a meteorologist?"

"Yes."

"Of course. I shall need you."

"Thank you! I have already begun charting our course."

Yonne put his arm around him in admiration. "You're a Vinibin after my own heart!"

Eroscheen interrupted. "You should know the truth, Sir Yonne. You are inviting all but certain death."

"Death?" he replied with grim humor. He glanced at Bornabi. "Immortality, you mean."

Bornabi smiled wanly.

Yonne's mind was on the job before him. He spoke quickly to Eroscheen. "If I can be shown the way, my plane will approach the island at an altitude far above all weather conditions. How far is Humshine from here?"

"Over 7,000 miles," said Eroscheen. "It is on the other half of the hemisphere."

"7,000 miles!" He was calculating rapidly. "How far away do you estimate the storm?"

"Less than twenty-four hours by the last report ten minutes ago."

Yonne whistled. "We must hurry!"

They all went down to the hangar. It was the first time that anyone but Vergia had come to view the plane, so completely was Yonne's privacy respected. The Chieftains watched him as he went over the mechanical parts. They were careful not to disturb him, and kept themselves at a distance, pointing out to each other different things about the craft and discussing them in great earnest.

But Eroscheen was continuously at his side. He brought him samples of fuel from large tanks that had been deposited on the beach. To Yonne's delight, not only one but all of them ignited to perfection. Eroscheen had already worked out many of the problems of distance, direction and height, based upon Vinibin knowledge of atmospheric conditions, and Yonne now checked these with him. He found the mathematics correct and smilingly patted Eroscheen on the back.

"I see you know your stuff! For the rest, we shall have to depend upon luck!"

Yonne asked for an hour to himself. He knew the venture was hazardous. He thought of Vergia and wondered if he would ever see her again. With a sinking feeling he forced his mind away from her and proceeded to complete his preparations. He wanted to be sure that Vinibins had adequate information from which to construct their own planes, should anything happen to him and Eroscheen. He therefore gathered up what literature he had in the plane on aeronautics, including some blueprints and diagrams of the craft itself. He translated hurriedly into Vinibin the instrument data of his flight to Vinibus, then wrapped everything carefully in a package.

* * * * *

Before the hour was up, the plane was being rolled out upon the beach. Yonne took Bornabi to one side, and gave him the package.

"Let Vergia open it—just in case we don't get back."

"It will be done as you say, Sir Yonne."

Yonne smiled with youthful determination. "I fully expect to be back!"

Bornabi took both his hands in his own. "We all expect you, and we shall be thinking of you every minute."

"One more thing, Bornabi. Tell Vergia I love her."

* * * * *

There was a quick and simple parting. Yonne and Eroscheen embraced the Chieftains. Kooklwucs was there too, jumping up and down and braying with excitement. Then, with a great roar of its motors, the plane moved across the sand, and turned seaward for the island of Humshine.

X

They sailed high over the shoreland of Quiloth, over its rolling hills, its fields and woodlands, then headed out to sea in a steady climb toward the stratosphere. They traveled for hours through clear, starlit skies, with no sign of the storm.

Yonne pressed the ship hard. So far, all had gone well.

Both he and Eroscheen knew, however, that the real test was yet to come—the landing through the Kommschein storm.

When the first pale streamers of dawn appeared they were approaching the great Kommschein sea.

"It won't be long now," said Eroscheen. "If the air remains clear, I'll be able to show you the island of Humshine."

They began to descend only to discover great cloud formations below and signs of the storm.

"Looks like we're staying up," said Yonne.

Eroscheen nodded. They sped on through the calm stratosphere rapidly cutting the distance between them and the island. For another hour they flew in silence. Then Eroscheen's eyes began to sparkle. He sat beside Yonne with an almost cocky spirit serenely confident in his hero from Earth. At last, he exclaimed: "Sir Yonne—we're there!"

"Over Dilphon's Refuge?"

"Yes." His eyes were glued to the chart. "According to my calculations——"

"It will be your calculations, Eroscheen, or none," said Yonne with a grim smile. "We're going down."

Imagine their delight when they came into the lower atmosphere to behold the island of Dilphon's Refuge below, radiant and serene in the sunlight of a peaceful sky!

The storm? It had never struck. Instead, they found a gentle summer breeze coaxing the waves lightly into the shores of Humshine. Far to the west they could see the fringe of black clouds, but it was clearly receding. The typhoon had missed the island by many miles.

Without mishap, with perfect timing, they had arrived at their destination precisely at the hour Eroscheen had figured.

They were flying at a high altitude, and the Chieftains had not seen them.

"Shall we try the beach for a landing?" asked Yonne.

"It will not be necessary," said Eroscheen.

"No?"

"You can see, Sir Yonne, the storm has passed far from the island."

"Yes—there was never any danger."

"Would you mind if we did not land?"

Yonne looked up in surprise.

"There is no need," said Eroscheen, "to disturb the Chieftains now that they are safe."

"You are certain they are safe?"

"Yes."

"Then, let's make for home!" cried Yonne, letting out a "Yippe!" Eroscheen laughed.

It had loomed up as such a dangerous undertaking; it turned out to be a calm, uneventful cruise—and one not even necessary!

They started back in high spirits, Yonne promptly forgetting about the Chieftains and dreaming of Vergia. Eroscheen sat at the cabin window, gazing with joy upon the scenes below. He was happy too; happy for his share in the rescue venture; happy in the knowledge of what new joys this aerial experience would add to the life of Vinibins. With his thoughts at ease now, the sensation of his first flight left him quite beyond words. He remained reverently absorbed in the wonders of aviation.

More to himself than to Eroscheen, Yonne said:

"How does one ask for a girl's hand upon Vinbus?"

Eroscheen looked up quizzically, then smiled. "You are thinking of Vergia?"

"Yes."

He grinned. "She has told me of your love."

"Does it seem strange to you?"

"Does what seem strange?"

"That we . . . a man from Earth, and Vergia should so quickly fall in love."

Eroscheen mused. "If you were to fall in love with a woman upon Earth, Sir Yonne, would it seem strange if she came from a faraway land?"

"What an old sage you are!" declared Yonne laughingly. "I suppose that would make me love her even more, wouldn't it."

"Perhaps."

"We have an old saying on Earth that distance lends enchantment." said Yonne.

"Then thirty million miles ought to make you and Vergia hopelessly in love with each other!"

They both laughed, and Yonne asked: "Do you see any reason then why we shouldn't get married?"

"Married?" Eroscheen didn't understand.

"Married," said Yonne emphasizing the word for clarity and going to some lengths at explanation.

"You see, I want to marry her."

Eroscheen did not see.

"Surely, Eroscheen, Vinibins have arrangements for marriage."

The young Vinibin's eyes suddenly brightened. "Oh—I think I see."

"Then what am I to do? You must tell me. I know nothing of your customs."

"What are you to do?" The serious expression had left Eroscheen's face and gave way to a mischievous one. "What would you do on Earth?"

"On Earth? Well, I should know exactly what to do."

"You will do the same on Vinibus. You will tell her of your love! You will——"

"Yes, I know, but then what?"

"Then what?" Eroscheen whistled roguishly.

"The ceremony," Yonne persisted, "the regulations . . . the law. How do I go about it?"

Eroscheen's face lit up. "Oh that. I am sure that can be taken care of in due time afterwards at the proper bureau in Quiloth."

"Afterwards?"

"Yes—after you and Vergia have a mind again to think of the practical side of living." In a serious tone he added, "Bornabi will be glad to explain the routine to you."

"The routine? Afterwards? But Eroscheen, you don't understand."

"Oh, yes I do!" he declared. "You and Vergia will know soon enough what your future plans will be."

"But now, before those plans can be made."

"Now?" He slapped Yonne heartily on the shoulder. In a solemn tone he said: "Now, Sir Yonne, you will love and coo as lovers do . . . ahem! . . . and at some future date, maybe, you will honor us by bestowing upon Vinibus some little Sir Yonnes and Vergias."

Yonne wasn't in a mood for humor. He sat silent for a while wondering why he couldn't make himself clear. But as Eroscheen continued to chide him good-naturedly, he began to sense that things were indeed quite clear. Wasn't this what he had been told at the Eternal Circle? Marriage— or its equivalent—upon Vinibus was an understanding between two people, a pledge, free from all legalistic considerations of property as we know them, free from economic dependence of one person upon the other. Marriage stood or fell upon the unburdened volition of both lovers. Like the tryst of the Gylu birds, it was——

* * * * *

For a while there was little further conversation. Each was absorbed in his own thoughts. Then Eroscheen checked the instrument readings against his chart, and said excitedly:

"Less than half the distance to go!"

"Are we over land?"

"Yes."

"It would be wonderful," mused Yonne, "if we could communicate the good news at once to Quiloth. On Earth we could radio Bornabi directly from the plane. You Vinibins must learn that science too."

"That ought not be difficult," said Eroscheen. "We need only apply those principles to air navigation that we have already developed for land and water."

"You can transmit messages to distant parts of the globe?"

"Oh yes." There was a look of boyish pride on his face. "Yes, we can do so as quickly as you and I can speak together here."

"Fine! Why can't we make a landing now and send a message to Bornabi?"

"We can. We are probably not far from one of our continental arteries." He consulted his chart again. "I shall be able to point it out to you when we drop within sight of land."

"You mean a telegraph office—a place from which we can dispatch the news?"

"Oh, yes, we can use it for that."

"Let's go!" cried Yonne eager for a chance to talk to Bornabi—perhaps to Vergia.

He nosed the plane downward. But this time they were taking too much for granted. As they came into the lower atmosphere, they were caught off guard. In their preoccupation with more pleasant things, they had forgotten all about the storm, and before they knew it, they were heading directly into a raging hurricane, such a one as they thought they would strike en route to the island!

"Oh," groaned Eroscheen, "I should have thought of this."

"I think we can pull out of it," said Yonne, but before he had uttered the words, a howling wind caught the plane and spun it around like a scrap of paper. In the flash of a moment, Yonne lost all control. Powerful air currents tossed them about with a violence that made the craft quiver dangerously.

Through it all, Eroscheen, strapped in his seat, looked inquiringly but calmly at Yonne. He seemed to be curious in an objective way only, to see how Yonne was going to handle the situation!

They were yet in clear atmosphere with the sun visible overhead. But to all sides and below them, giant clouds were being lashed into grotesque shapes. The ship trembled like a frightened thing as descending eddies violently gripped its frame and sucked it down into the storm.

Yonne called to Eroscheen to keep a close vigil for sight of land. But visibility was zero, and there was slight prospect of seeing anything before a crash. Then Yonne heard the sound of ripping metal and saw with horror that one wing was being torn from the fuselage. The plane plunged downward. Even the complacent Eroscheen sensed danger, and his face took on a look of concern.

A crash seemed inevitable. Yonne felt an easy sense of abandon, a feeling of total irresponsibility. Irrelevant pictures arose before him, pictures that loomed out of the subconscious like the final résumé of a life span coming to its close. His whole conscious being seemed to seek escape from the scene of disaster, from the imminent dissolution of the body.

He was startled out of his fixation with death by the voice of Eroscheen:

"Sir Yonne! The rain! The wind has stopped!"

In some miraculous way, the plane, after having fallen far into the atmosphere, had righted itself. Eroscheen exclaimed again:

"I see the artery!"

"The what?"

"There . . . the artery."

Through the murky air he pointed out a narrow ridge that looked more like a black pencil line drawn against the gray background of mist than solid earth. As they descended they could see its outline and also the surrounding lower land.

Yonne was still breathing hard from the fright of only seconds ago. He alone knew how close they had both been to disaster. He couldn't believe they were flying smoothly again through calm air.

They landed in a flat grain field. Bumping precariously over the soft ground, the plane came to a halt, the drooping wing still clinging faithfully to the fuselage! Unperturbed, Eroscheen jumped to the ground and looked at the plane.

"Too bad," he said sadly, "the ship has been damaged."

"That's an understatement if ever there was one!" declared Yonne wiping the sweat from his face. The wing was so badly twisted out of line it was a mystery how it had remained a functioning part of the plane. "Well," he said grimly, "we may not have saved the Chieftains, but we surely saved ourselves—and by a narrow squeak!"

They scrutinized the wing. "It does not appear serious, does it?" said Eroscheen regarding Yonne inquiringly.

"I'm afraid it does." Yonne was wondering what their chances would be of repairing it.

"We can fix it at the artery," said Eroscheen.

"At the artery?"

"Yes."

"The damage is pretty bad."

"We can fix it," repeated Eroscheen more positively. "I am sure of it."

Through the fog and rain they could faintly see the "artery." It appeared to be a narrow, raised structure running in a curved line like a huge viaduct. Yonne could discern objects darting swiftly along the top of it.

"Your transportation system?"

Eroscheen nodded. "They are more than that. We call them arteries because they are the life-streams of our communities." He smiled knowingly. "You will see."

Through torrents of rain they set out for the artery some few miles away. On approaching, Yonne noticed that what seemed at first to be only an elevated right-of-way for transportation was in reality a more complicated structure. About 150 feet in height, with oddly designed architecture, it might have been taken at a distance for the ramparts of a fortress on a festive day. On closer view, it proved to be a row of streamlined buildings bedecked for some holiday occasion. It ran in either direction as far as the eye could see.

They came out upon a wide thoroughfare. Vinibins were busily going to and fro in a steady stream.

"This," said Eroscheen, "is the Socio of Krixlrem." With a wave of his hand, he added, "The artery is the center of local activity where we carry on primary production, communication and transportation."

Yonne did not expect so soon to get a glimpse of a Vinibin rural community as he supposed this would be, and he was curious. He surveyed the elongated structure. The style varied markedly every few hundred yards, each section containing some productive enterprise. One part looked strikingly like a modern bank building, with straight classic lines and massive walls. But the architecture was truly functional, not psychological as in the case of a bank build-

159

ing on Earth. It housed the productive machinery of a heavy local industry. Another section followed a warm graceful pattern. Its walls were a smooth creamy white like our adobe houses of the southwest, and it had numerous balconies with red tile roofs and oddly designed terraces. Yes, it was a restaurant where Vinibins ate during the production periods.

There was a stretch of some two hundred yards carrying out the tree colonnade design of Bornabi's home, and one with large horizontal, streamlined pieces like the timber of a giant log cabin. These housed the communication and transportation centers for the Socio.

They stood for a moment taking in the scene.

Yonne's eye was attracted to the busy thoroughfare. It was a business lane, to be sure, but it had none of the hectic bustle of our typical urban streets. There was, in fact, a lazy, Andalusian atmosphere. There were no vehicles of any kind; no shrill traffic whistles or street cars. There was no piercing sound of wheels on metal tracks; none of the familiar din and noise of our own industrial life. Everyone moved briskly; but there was an over-all slowness of tempo quite out of keeping with the best metropolitan practices on Earth.

They came to the streamlined building. "Here is where we will send our message," said Eroscheen.

They entered by a broad flight of stairs and came into a lobby extending the width of the artery—a width equal to a city block. The lobby, spacious and elegant, had high, arched ceilings and wide corridors into which streamed pale shafts of light from unseen points. One got the impression of being in a typically modern and not altogether unworldly kind of place. Yonne was, in fact, quite pleasantly reminded of some of the finer types of Earthly business establishments.

They entered one of the corridors leading into a large circular room attended by a young male Vinibin. Along the walls were rows of small compartments with doors.

"We shall secure our connection here," said Eroscheen.

Wishing to remain unnoticed, Yonne proposed they do their visiting incognito. "It will facilitate things for the time being," he said.

Eroscheen nodded, and spoke to the attendant.

He presented a card from which the young Vinibin made some entries on a metal plate before him.

"The charge?"

"Personal," said Eroscheen putting the card back in his pocket.

"Verbal or code?"

Eroscheen reflected a moment then answered, "Code."

"You may connect on line 8," said the clerk. "It is open."

They were directed to one of the alcoves along the wall. The simple, businesslike procedure made Yonne feel that he was back on Earth. Eroscheen hastened to explain:

"In all personal service transactions, Sir Yonne, we require certain identifying information, as you have seen. I am making this a personal call; so it has to be distinguished by the attendant from one chargeable to productive operation. In the latter case I should have had to identify the production unit and present an order from it against which the charge would then have been placed."

Another familiar Earthly touch!

Yonne's curiosity was heightened by the implications all this suggested in the novel Vinibin scheme of things. Eroscheen elaborated on the routine of this incident.

"Generally, we communicate verbally or in code. The code method is less costly and serves well enough for all simple messages. Where involved situations are under discussion, however, the verbal transmission is preferable because it enables us to enter more intimately into the points under consideration."

Yonne nodded smilingly, amused at the thoroughly human pattern of things.

They came to the booth. A white flash indicated to Eroscheen that the connection was made. He turned to Yonne.

"What shall I say, Sir Yonne?"

"Say that we found the Chieftains safe and that the storm missed the island."

"And our own mishap?"

"You said the damage can be readily repaired?"

"Yes."

"Then why mention it. No need to worry them. We can explain after we return."

"Very well." Eroscheen started to enter the booth then stopped as though he were not altogether satisfied that the message was complete. There was the slightest twinkle in his eye. But he said nothing and sat at the desk provided for sending the code. He wrote some symbols again on a metal plate, using a pointed instrument shaped like a pencil which he carried with him. When he had finished he returned it to his pocket and regarded Yonne questioningly.

"You are sure there is nothing else you wish to say, Sir Yonne?"

Yes, there was something. But he hestitated to make the request not wishing to put Eroscheen to unnecessary expense. Eroscheen's alert, boyish eyes understood.

"Come," he said, "I have a surprise for you." He took Yonne by the arm and they walked back to the clerk's desk.

"What is it?"

"You would like to talk to Vergia?"

Yonne's beaming face was answer enough!

"But not in code," suggested Eroscheen with a chuckle.

"You are very discerning!"

"It shall be done! A message to Vergia is quite as important as anything we have to do!"

The clerk greeted them smilingly.

"Another message?"

"Yes," Yonne spoke up eagerly.

"For yourself?"

"Yes."

"Your card, please."

Yonne fumbled about in his pockets. Eroscheen laughed.

"My friend does not have his card," he said. "Please enter it against mine."

The clerk obligingly made the necessary notation.

"A private, verbal connection this time," said Eroscheen, "to Vergia, daughter of Bornabi, Socio Quiloth."

"Line 5 is available," said the clerk.

They entered a large, oval-shaped chamber. Like the previous one, it had a series of compartments along the walls, but these were much larger, and all had numbered doors. Eroscheen escorted Yonne into one. It was bare of all furnishings except for a few lounging chairs which faced a white semicircular wall opposite the entrance.

"If you wish," said Eroscheen, "you can talk to Vergia while I make inquiry as to the needed repairs for the plane. The initial time allowance is five minutes, but if you want to extend it you may do so by pressing this." He indicated a button underneath the arm of the chair.

"Five minutes is quite enough," Yonne said gratefully.

"All right. All you need to do is to sit in this chair. After you close the door you will have to wait for the flash of white light at the upper portion of the wall in front of you. It will be a signal that contact has been made."

It was all quite simple.

"Give Vergia my greetings," said Eroscheen as he left. "I'll be back shortly."

Yonne waited for the signal and pondered the situation. These signs of Vinibin mechanical advancement made him feel just a little disappointed. First he had supposed Vinibins to be a very backward people, now he half expected against his better judgment, to find weird devices or processes unthinkable to human beings. Instead, everything was falling quite naturally into place, and things seemed to proceed upon the laws of physics and chemistry as he knew them on Earth, and there was no room either for magic or wizardry.

His musings were interrupted by the white light. Then, as though coming from somewhere in the room, a voice announced:

"You are connected. Vergia will speak to you."

Yonne waited. Gradually the light faded and it grew dark. But the room was flooded at once with an even light as bright as day. Then something incredible happened. Yonne felt a giddy sensation as though he were being lifted bodily out of the place. The walls seemed to recede. He saw the room being transformed as if by magic into the antechamber of Bornabi's house! Before him in one of the rustic chairs, sat Vergia!—Vergia, looking lovelier than ever, sitting right beside him in the same room! All about them were the familiar objects of the little dome-shaped room where he had first met her and Bornabi.

He was mystified. What had happened? Had he been magically whisked away 3,000 miles back to her?

Vergia smiled and rose from her chair to greet him. He rushed forward with outstretched hands.

"Vergia!"

"Yonne!" she cried in delight. "You are safe!"

164

Her slender figure stood exquisitely erect before him. There was an eager, wistful look in her face. Impulsively, she extended her hands to him.

"Oh, Yonne," she cried, "it is wonderful—about you and the Chieftains." The tender light in her deep, soft eyes spoke of gratitude and love. She sighed with pleasure, and Yonne yearned to clasp her in his arms.

Unconsciously, he had walked to meet her when suddenly his finger tips touched the wall! He was frightened. What was this? Was he dreaming? No! It could not be . . . it must not be! Startled, he cried alond, "Vergia, darling! Are you really here?"

"Of course I am here," she said, her smiling figure still before him, "to talk to you, although my body is 3,000 miles away."

"Three thousand miles away!"

"Yes."

Instantly, he saw it all. He had been deceived by a perfect technique of television and had mistaken a three dimensional photographic likeness for reality itself.

"Then we are really not together yet?"

"Not yet, dearest. You know that, don't you, Yonne?"

"Yes . . . of course."

His bewilderment caused her to look more closely, and she became alarmed.

"Yonne!"

Yonne stared.

"You are pale!" she cried.

He surveyed himself and noticed his drenched and disheveled clothing. He laughed. "I am all right. We were caught in a heavy rain."

She breathed a sigh of relief.

He wanted to kiss her for her concern.

"Vergia . . . dearest!" he murmured.

"Yonne, darling, I love you! I can say it now. Oh, I'm sure of it . . . I love you!"

Yonne pressed his lips against the wall and his hands against the image of hers. Murmuring his love, he stood gazing upon her. The minutes passed. They remained standing, lost to everything but the consciousness of their love. The white light in the room flickered; the image faded. But he knew this time it was real!

The room darkened and lighted again. In a daze, he walked out of the compartment directly into the arms of Eroscheen, almost knocking him over.

"Great Vinibus!" exclaimed Eroscheen, balancing himself after the collision. "What has happened?"

"We're returning to Vergia at once!"

"At once? Is anything wrong?"

"Wrong?" Yonne hugged him. "Everything couldn't be more right! Oh, my precious, Vergia!" and he hugged Eroscheen again as he danced him around.

"I told you," said Eroscheen in boyish fun, "thirty million miles would make a bad case for you."

"Very bad," admitted Yonne.

"Control yourself," said Eroscheen shaking his head with feigned earnestness.

"But I don't want to!" declared Yonne exuberantly.

"Come," Eroscheen linked his arm into Yonne's. "I will soon have your mind on other things."

They started for another part of the building. Yonne didn't know where they were going, and he didn't care. He wanted only to think of Vergia, of her gentle face, her soft voice, her enticing figure as it stood there before him on the screen.

"How long will it take?" he asked.

"To fix the ship?"

"Yes."

"We shall soon find out. An engineer is on his way."

"So quickly?"

"He is probably waiting for us."

They hurried on—through more lobbies, more corridors. More circular rooms! More compartments! At last they entered one resembling a large passenger elevator. Eroscheen took out his metal instrument and inserted the point into a number of small openings in the wall.

"The magic pencil!" said Yonne.

"Yes. This should take us near the spot."

The door closed, and Yonne could feel an accelerating motion downward. They swerved, then went rapidly forward along a subway.

"For short distances," said Eroscheen, "we use these subterranean conveyors in every Socio."

Yonne nodded. He was about to add that humans also had such systems of transportation on Earth, when he noticed a frown on Eroscheen's face.

"We don't exactly like them," said Eroscheen. "They remain with us, a necessary evil."

"They seem effective."

"Perhaps—but we prefer to be above ground where it is bright and sunny."

Yonne smiled. "Don't you use vehicles on land?"

"Rarely. We generally go on horse or foot. Long journeys are made above the artery."

"Above the artery?"

"Yes. You will see when we ride in one on the way to the manufactory where the plane is to be fixed."

There was an upward turn of the conveyor as it brought them back to the surface. The door opened, and Yonne saw that they were out in the open country again. The little stopping point from which they emerged was snugly hidden by trees and foliage. The plane was discernible not a quarter of a mile away.

"Excellent service!" declared Yonne.

The compliment pleased Eroscheen. They noticed that someone had already arrived at the plane, and hurried on. A stalwart young Vinibin was making a rough sketch of the damaged parts. Seeing them, he bowed graciously. Eroscheen introduced him:

"Sir Yonne, this is Elan-Coli, ranking metallurgist in Krixlrem and one of its famous music critics, too."

"A craftsman *and* a critic?" Yonne started in surprise again then quickly checked himself. "Of course . . . of course," he hastened to add and gave the newcomer the sweeping Vinibin bow.

Elan-Coli returned the greeting but stared at him in wonder. Like Eroscheen, he was awe-stricken.

"We are deeply grateful, Sir Yonne," he said, "that you and your wonderful ship were not destroyed by the Komm-schein storms."

Yonne looked at Eroscheen who stood by smiling guiltily and shrugging his shoulders. "I didn't talk—the ship did!" he said.

Elan-Coli continued: "Eroscheen has told me your wishes. We shall keep your presence a secret."

"Thank you," said Yonne.

Together, they surveyed the quick sketch Elan-Coli had made. Yonne found it to be accurate, showing precisely the construction of the damaged parts. Elan-Coli did some estimating on a separate sheet of paper. Looking up from his figures, he said:

"We shall have no difficulty in restoring the broken parts. You will be able to resume your flight in one or two days."

168

"That long?" exclaimed Yonne forgetting that but a moment ago he thought the part could not be repaired.

Elan-Coli looked apologetic. "We have no such ships, Sir Yonne. We must fashion special dies."

Yonne realized how unreasonable he was in his eagerness to get back to Vergia. His impatience made Elan-Coli think humans could perform magic, while Yonne doubted if he could have had the job done nearly as fast on Earth.

"Two days is excellent time," he said.

Elan-Coli smiled gratefully. He conferred hurriedly with Eroscheen, who showed him his card from which he made some notations. Eroscheen said: "Charge it to the Socio of Quiloth. I am sure the province will feel honored."

Elan-Coli bowed, and they left him to finish his work. Returning to the subway compartment, they were carried back to the artery.

"If you wish," said Eroscheen, "we can return at once to Quiloth by way of the artery and come back to get the plane when it is finished."

Yonne was greatly tempted. On second thought, however, he decided this would be unwise. He wanted to inspire Vinibin confidence in aviation—to demonstrate on the occasion of this first test the fullest capacity of aviation not its limitations. Were he to return to Quiloth leaving a broken plane behind it would mar the experience. He wanted two things to stand out: that he had outwitted by means of aviation the worst storm of the Kommschein sea and that he landed successfully and returned home safely despite the serious damage to the plane.

His longing for Vergia had to be subdued for a little while.

Eroscheen's face lit up with an idea.

"I could take you visiting, Sir Yonne, while the plane is being fixed."

"Visiting?"

"Yes. We could go to some of our manufactories, our conveyors. We might even have time to visit the Youth Community of this Socio."

"Fine!" said Yonne.

"Then we shall first have something to eat," said Eroscheen with gusto. "I'm famished!"

"Good. That little experience can be the first stop on our itinerary."

Eroscheen's youthful face shone. By this time he had already read Yonne's true reactions to Vinibin achievements, and knew he was impressed. "I will enjoy this almost as much as you," he declared, "just for the fun of seeing what you will think of us."

Yonne laughed. "You have already given me much to think about."

"Yes?"

"But aren't you a little afraid?" said Yonne coyly.

"Afraid—of what?"

"Of what my judgment will be?"

Eroscheen's eyes twinkled with laughter. "No." he said, "I think I know what it will be."

XI

They stopped for lunch in the building with the white walls and red balconies. Since it was already late morning, primary production was over, so they met few Vinibins.

Eroscheen selected one of the smaller balconies overlooking the thoroughfare. It was a cozy place, with a table for two.

The weather had cleared, and they had an excellent view of the country beyond the Socio. Through the tropical foliage they could see portions of Vinibin dwelling places like Bornabi's scattered over the countryside like pieces of bric-a-brac glistening in the sunlight.

There were nonresidential buildings, too. These housed local Aesthetic Production and Adult Education classes.

A group of buildings, some distance from the others, caught Yonne's attention. It covered a wide area and appeared to be enclosed by a miniature artery.

"That is the Youth Community," said Eroscheen. "You can always tell it by the artery that encircles or separates it from the rest of the community. It is a replica on a small scale of the entire Vinibin plan of community life. Within the artery are the educational laboratories for primary production; above, are the conveyors that serve as transportation. The central buildings and grounds comprise the training quarters for the aesthetic and recreational development of Vinibin youth.

"A university campus," suggested Yonne.

The remark missed Eroscheen. He was in gay spirits as he regarded his Earthly guest across the table.

"Let us call for our food," he said. "We can talk about things while we wait." He took out his little metal pencil.

Yonne looked about. No one came to serve them.

"Tell me what you would like," Eroscheen urged, "and I shall be glad to get it for you."

"Please—if we are to serve ourselves, I want to help."

Eroscheen smiled and shook his head. He pointed to the pencil. "This will serve us."

"That?"

"Yes."

He inserted the point in a small opening at the side of the table, and the top became illuminated with a graphic representation of the dishes available for the day. Yonne laughed at the ingenious device. A true photographic likeness of the food was displayed by this electric menu just as it was to be served. Most items were unfamiliar to Yonne, and he chose only those dishes which he already knew. But Eroscheen eagerly selected an assortment drawn together from all parts of the illuminated table.

"It is great fun," he said, "to try new dishes when you are in strange places—just to test the skill of the dietician."

The food was ordered via the magic pencil, and Eroscheen extinguished the menu.

"This *is* going to be fun," declared Yonne. He looked down upon the Vinibin thoroughfare. "I suppose this is an important Vinibin Socio—judging from the sizeable nature of the establishments here in the artery."

"All Socios are equally important," said Eroscheen simply. "They produce nearly everything that is needed for local use."

"I know," said Yonne, eager to display what he had learned at the Cypress Grove. "You Vinibins have no very large industrial establishments."

"No. Surpluses beyond Socio use are produced only in accordance with a policy of even exchange between provinces for goods not readily available in all parts of the globe. So far as the establishments you see here are concerned, you will find them with some variation to extend throughout the length of the entire artery. They constitute the characteristic chain which *is* the artery. Along it flows the stream of Vinibin collective life. Would you like to have me tell you some things about it before we visit the establishments?"

"Yes."

"Well, the artery at which we now find ourselves happens to be one of the eight major or global chains; that is, it extends across the entire hemisphere from pole to pole.

172

There are many other smaller arteries, but these large ones have a right of way nearly 12,000 miles. They are connected with each other and with the shorter parallel arteries by thousands of crossway systems. Between them they knit together all the lands of Vinibus into a vast network of communication, transportation and production. An artery, no matter where you find it, is a vital channel between all Vinibin communities. Within its structure you will see all the important collective or primary Vinibin enterprises, from the active producing and coordinating agencies to the granaries and warehouses. Along the top of the artery the conveyors speed to carry Vinibins and surplus produce to near and distant points. On the land between arteries are the resident communities, the Socios and their aesthetic institutions; also between are the farms, the timber lands, the natural resources."

Eroscheen was interrupted by the sound of a musical gong. "Ah! dinner is being served," he said, swallowing with pleasant anticipation.

But no one came to serve it. Yonne heard a faint rustle along the wall nearest the table. A sliding panel the size of their table top removed itself silently from the wall, and there, in an opening like that of a small cabinet, stood their dinner, steaming and delicious-looking. Yonne was about to get up and bring it to their table. Eroscheen restrained him. "It will come."

It did come. The entire shelf on which the food was placed now moved smoothly towards them on a thin horizontal shaft until it was just above the table, then slid snugly over the top. With a click the shaft disengaged itself, receded into the wall and disappeared. Eroscheen chuckled at Yonne's look of surprise. They served themselves from containers fitted into depressions in the tray to which Eroscheen was always careful to replace them after they had emptied the contents. The food was good, but Yonne hardly knew what he was eating in his preoccupation with the mechanics of the situation. Not an ordinary automat was this, but the acme of technological finesse, the dream of silent, superb mechanical service come to reality. Struck by the humor of the thing, Yonne asked laughingly.

"Who will remove and wash the dirty dishes?"

"Oh, they will be removed simply enough—much in the same way that they came. And they will be washed too. Many things will happen to complete the process."

"But who does all the work?"

"That is mechanical and automatic," said Eroscheen. "The only direct Vinibin services are those of the dietician who compiles the quantity formulas. And that is a real responsibility! Then, there are the manual and technical skills of operating and supervising the complicated machinery."

"Not bad!" said Yonne whistling admiringly.

* * * * *

They tarried a while on the little balcony. There were so many things Yonne wanted to know.

"Do you charge yourself for the services we have been receiving?" he asked.

"Yes."

"But why do you do this when everything is . . . well . . . free, I guess."

Eroscheen looked puzzled, but he answered him adequately enough.

"Our social wealth is naturally a limited thing, Sir Yonne, and it is dependent upon Vinibin creative effort. It is not spontaneously available in limitless quantities like the air we breathe. We must, therefore, plan both the productive efforts that meet our needs, and the utilization of the wealth we have created. This requires much accounting, and many Vinibins are engaged in this service alone. Each Socio, for example, shares equitably in the total Vinibin produce, against which it draws for its residents, charging the allowances to each individual's account. Before doing this, however, the Socio first sets aside a predetermined amount for nonpersonal services like transportation, sanitation, health, etc. These costs are not chargeable to an individual because they must be maintained as a common resource regardless of individual need. After they and some other allowances for common Socio requirements are set aside on a quarter-year accounting basis, the remainder— and by far the major portion—of the Socio's share, accrues to the individual's personal account. The card which you saw me present is honored for my personal services no matter where I go. The charge is always reverted to my resident Socio if I avail myself of services elsewhere."

"A sort of planetary credit system," Yonne suggested.

"Yes, I believe you can call it that."

"But what happens if you overdraw your account?"

Eroscheen grimaced.

"One tries not do do that. But still, should it happen, the overdraft is applied against one's succeeding quarterly allowance. More often, however, we do not draw out to the full our personal resources in any one quarter."

"Then what happens to what you have left at the end of the quarter?"

"Oh, that is a resource which you may wish to accumulate over a period of time for exceptional purposes. Right now, I am saving to get a new type of seagoing motorboat in which I want to make some trips to remote regions of the Kommschein Sea. That is an ambition many of us Vinibins have."

"Oh!" Yonne smiled at this evidence of personal capitalism. "But if you die, what becomes of your savings?"

"They are not lost, of course. They revert to the Socio from whence they came."

"Hm! One more question . . . this long distance conversation I had with Vergia. Is such service readily available for everyone?"

"Oh yes."

"Isn't it a great social expense?"

"Quite the contrary. When it was first developed many years ago it did involve great cost. But now it is both an economy and a convenience. For one thing, it has greatly reduced long distance transportation costs, to say nothing about the time it has saved. Before the 'pictaudis'—that is what we call it—Vinibins could not converse with friends far away and be in their very presence, without first making long and expensive journeys. That is no longer necessary. And, since the use of the pictaudis constitutes a personal charge while transportation is a collective one, it is an additional social saving. "But," he added, "all this is not the most important value of the pictaudis. It is in production that we find its greatest use. Every productive unit has a pictaudis room for conference purposes. It is readily connectible with the conference rooms of other units. These rooms operate on a very simple principle. One half of a conference table is placed flush against a projecting screen or wall. When contact with another establishment is made, the 'half rooms' of the two agencies become as one, and the two table halves and their occupants likewise are joined, one portion being real and the other a photographic likeness of the distant unit. The conferees can thus sit around a table, as it were, to discuss and work out their production problems just as though they were actually together in the flesh when, in fact, they may be thousands of miles apart."

Yonne shook his head and chuckled. "And I thought . . . !"

"What did you think, Sir Yonne?"

"Never mind. Tell me more."

"What shall I tell you?"

"This credit system—does it mean that everyone gets the same credit or pay, regardless of the nature of his work? Aren't some services more important than others?"

"I don't know if I quite understand you," replied Eroscheen. "Some things are more important than others, of course . . . the basic manual services, for instance."

"The what?"

"The basic manual services. They cannot always be replaced by automatic devices. And there are not so many of them left! They are of great actual and moral importance to us—the most important of all the services, Sir Yonne."

"The most important? But that is contrary to——" Yonne hesitated.

"Contrary to what?" asked Eroscheen.

He was going to say "contrary to the human attitude," but he thought better of it. "Manual tasks" he said instead, "are quite simple to be accorded such distinction."

"Simple?" Eroscheen studied Yonne for a moment. "Well, that may be so. But it is their very simplicity that constitutes a challenge to our imagination. The simple, manual task, you see, is the irreducible base of the refinements of contemporary social life. It is the fulcrum of the entire mechanical superstructure. The most complicated machine is impotent—a dead thing—without it. The highest technical skill is as nothing without it. Our culture, our leisure time, are nonexistent without it. Our whole civilization rests upon the simple manual act. It is the visible reminder that Vinibin bodily and mental energy are congealed in all our mechanical and technical achievements, that all things are fundamentally the product of these."

177

"And how do you express this importance of, ah . . . the simple manual act in . . . well, in everyday life?"

"That is easily explained, Sir Yonne. Only special merit in aesthetic and educational performance entitles one to the fullest participation in the basic manual tasks. Of course, no one is completely left out. This privilege . . ."

Yonne put up his hand with a grin, "Wait!—I know that every Vinibin performs a multiple of manual and mental services. But why bestow such honor upon the simple manual task?"

"Because, Sir Yonne, we have learned that the privilege of sharing in basic manual tasks assures mental balance. As Dilphon-Mosa once said, 'it is like falling upon one's knees and kissing the soil of Vinibus.' "

Yonne grunted. Eroscheen tried to explain it another way:

"From the standpoint of production, every manual act carries with it an admission of mechanical limitation. In this respect it is a spur to inventive genius. For a Vinibin to come suddenly upon some new idea while performing the manual task, some improved, mechanical way of accomplishing it, is a pleasure seldom surpassed. And, paradoxically enough, it fixes upon the mind the important fact that manual labor is the irreducible medium through which its opposite, mental labor, can function creatively for the common good. Personal identification with it, therefore, is absolutely essential for the individual's complete social and productive orientation."

"An interesting view," said Yonne.

"An interesting fact," corrected Eroscheen.

Yonne smiled. "Does this mean then, that everyone gets the same remuneration?"

"Yes and no. Yes, if you understand by remuneration that everyone gets an equal share of the residue of social wealth, after common needs and the needs of youths and children

178

have been met by the Socio. But," he added hastily, "this does not mean that everyone makes the same use of his credit—his remuneration, if you will. The common necessities having first been provided for on a collective basis, the individual is free to use his personal credit as he pleases. And, just as there are wide differences in individuals, so are there wide and interesting differences in the way they expend their . . . ah, remuneration to gratify personal wants and desires."

To all this Yonne could only shake his head in disbelief. "You Vinibins are certainly an amazing people," he declared, "an amazingly good people."

Eroscheen thought Yonne was joking.

"Well, we are a much happier, if not a better people," he said laughingly, "than we once were. That much is true. But, in the main, I suppose we are not much different from our ancestors. New ethical considerations, new cultural backgrounds, order and mutualism in our collective life—all these have simply conditioned our thought processes and ideals in a different—let me say, a better way. That is the important thing."

"Perhaps," said Yonne looking meditatively out over the landscape. "But, surely, some of your people must commit wrongs against their fellows. How do you punish crime?"

"Punish crime?" asked Eroscheen. "That phrase, Sir Yonne, sounds like an echo from the distant past. Before Dilphon-Mosa, Vinibins talked much about crime and punishment. Today, these words have little meaning for us. When one removes the source of an infection, the disease disappears."

Yonne was still incredulous. "How did you remove the infection?"

"We have not removed it altogether. Individual misconduct still commands our attention, of course. But crime,

179

as our ancestors knew it, was a form of antisocial behavior quite peculiar to their own primitive society. The records of antiquity abound in illustrations on the subject.

"The cause, for example, was nearly always the primitive concept of title to property. This ancient, perversive institution stands out sharply in the light of historical perspective as the greatest single cause—almost the only cause! The social inequities it begot were the mainsprings of criminal tendency, for all too frequently it developed a mania for acquisition that drove Vinibins into every kind of criminal excess. Property was the parent of crime as it was the parent of thrift. Thrift or crime, these were the two ways to Vinibin success. When the unsuccessful individual was frustrated in his lust for property whether by lack of opportunity, skill, or cunning, there was always open to him the way of crime. And it was a tempting one too, when judged by the precedent of the times. Some of the greatest property holdings of antiquity were known to have been accumulated by liberal deviations from the path of righteousness. This precedence served both as an incentive and a justification to criminal offenders. It was a quick and often sure way of bridging the gap between material security and poverty, between social position and obscurity.

"In studying our old records, Sir Yonne, you will find that the commonest types of crime were those involving theft, forgery, larceny, extortion, robbery, and a thousand and one kinds of swindle in productive activity. The property motivation in every one of them is clear to us now. Today, the very idea of ownership, whether by the individual or the state, is repugnant to our deepest ethical considerations—to the whole concept of The Kinship of All Living Things. One does not acquire title to one's own kin! And upon Vinibus all things are endowed with the attributes of life and kinship. They are, thus, beyond the pale of property!

180

"Even from a practical standpoint," Eroscheen went on, "we have long ago discarded the notion of property title as being too petty, too limiting for any intelligent scheme of social intercourse. The notion clashes too violently with a smooth functioning of our whole production machinery."

He scrutinized Yonne from across the table. Yonne nodded without acquiescing. "I follow what you are saying," he said. "But, it doesn't seem plausible that all crime should be attributable solely to property. We on Earth know of crimes against the person, against sex, crimes of jealousy, crimes arising out of deep personal animosities . . . serious crimes, even murder."

"That is true," said Eroscheen. Such cases of misconduct also occur on Vinibus. Sometimes they reveal pathological disturbances requiring medical treatment. Sometimes, they are truly the result of malicious intent. Then we must resort to disciplinary measures."

"Really!" cried Yonne with unconcealed delight at this sign of Vinibin imperfection.

Eroscheen laughed good-naturedly.

"And how do you administer the discipline?"

"We have well-established procedures. The particular methods vary with every Socio."

"For example . . . ?"

"Well, take the Socio of Quiloth. Decision is generally rendered by a committee of the accused person's qualified peers."

"Ah, like our jury system on Earth," broke in Yonne.

"Yes?" queried Eroscheen.

"Sounds like it—but go on."

"Well, then, we Vinibins recognize, as no doubt you humans do, that no two offenses are the same and that there are many different avenues of behavior in which they are apt to be committed. No trial panel could ever judge intelligently in so great a variety of situations unless it is well informed in the particular behavior area concerned. For this reason, the accused and complainant, be they groups or individuals, first take their case to a jurisdiction referee for a ruling on two points: one, the broad field in which the case is to be heard and, two, the level at which it is to be set as a major or minor offense."

"At last something familiar!" declared Yonne pleasantly.

"I am glad," said Eroscheen and continued. "These two preliminaries agreed upon, the contending parties draw, from a local register, by lot and in turn, the prescribed number of names of available Vinibins qualified in the area in which the case is to be judged."

"Hm." Yonne nodded knowingly.

"As you may surmise, Sir Yonne, there are many different kinds of local registers of qualified Vinibins because there are many kinds of offenses and fields of Vinibin behavior—or, shall I say misbehavior?"

Yonne grinned.

"So, this becomes a most important department of adult education. Individual preparation for productive service on trial panels of necessity starts late in the education of every Vinibin. Some Vinibins become well versed in a number of related fields of conduct and so may be qualified for more than one register. Every Vinibin's qualifications for productive service on specific trial panels, however, are certified to by the appropriate Adult Education branch, and so——"

Yonne threw up his hands in protest and shook his head.

"What is it?" asked Eroscheen.

"We part company again," he said laughing.

"Why?"

"It's not the same."

"What's not the same?"

"Our jury system."

"Oh?"

"With you every Vinibin must be specially trained to serve on a trial panel?"

"Yes, every Vinibin who demonstrates ability for it."

"So everybody doesn't serve."

"Of course not—only those . . ."

". . . I know," laughed Yonne repeating the answer with him, "only those who qualify themselves. What would be a typical case?"

"Slander," said Eroscheen. "Let us assume that the Vinibin accused of this has been found guilty. The disciplinary verdict might, perhaps, call for his suspension from the performance of some basic productive service. He might be denied the privilege for a time of participating in a manual function for which he is qualified, like operating the mechanics of a heating plant, or servicing a machine for public sanitation, or tilling the soil . . ."

"What a strange punishment! And does that really do it?"

Eroscheen laughed at Yonne's question.

"Oh, that is a drastic discipline, Sir Yonne. I doubt if the trial committee would invoke it so readily as I am invoking it here in a purely hypothetical way—unless the case were really serious. To lose caste through such a verdict would be feared by any Vinibin. It would force him to accept primary production benefits without being allowed to share in their creation. He would be quite disgraced. No Vinibin would like that, believe me!"

"Incredible!" was all Yonne could say. Yet in his mind he was beginning to grope for what was so incredible about it. Upon reflection, he said:

"I had imagined you would call upon a more formal

state agency to deal with this problem. I was, in fact, coming to think that your scheme of things requires a highly complex kind of state. After all, the state——"

"The State?" inquired Eroscheen. "Why the State?"

Yonne started to elaborate on the human idea of the State, but Eroscheen soon shook his head vigorously.

"Oh, no, Sir Yonne, I don't think we have this kind of superstructure upon Vinibus. Many, many centuries ago before the time of Dilphon-Mosa we may have had something like it. I don't know. What we had then was a kind of political colossus which you may call the State. It weighed heavily upon all Vinibins. You can find the information in the records of Vinibin antiquity. Believe me, it will make you positively dizzy trying to fathom the countless laws and functions of this—well this ancient State: Statute books upon statute books; laws upon laws; a hierarchy of governmental divisions and departments, and courts, and bureaus—all of them reaching into the innermost recesses of personal life. I daresay the whole monstrous thing must have seemed bedlam to the individual of that day, especially since, as we know now, it contributed little or nothing to his genuine well-being. Yet, this ancient state was existent in the name of individualism, a queer kind of individualism that thrived on an atavistic idealism of savagery, yet depended on a tyranny of coersive regulations upon the individual to keep him from falling back completely into the savage state."

"Hm . . ." It all had a familiar ring! "This colossus of government," Yonne asked thinking of the human order of things, "how do you avoid it today?"

"Avoid it? We don't have to. It died a natural death when the parent that nourished it—property title in the individual or the state—expired. As you know, that happened when we came to understand the Kinship of All Living Things, and this marked the end of giantism in government

184

as it marked the end of giantism in production. This was to be expected since the property considerations in every individual and collective transaction had always constituted the chief concern of government. Furthermore, the state had been indispensable as an instrument to check the criminal tendencies inherent in the competitive struggle for the acquisition of property by individuals and even whole nations.

"In those ancient times, Sir Yonne, the political state had to be vested with a multitude of coercive powers, powers that were implied in the settlement of every civil or criminal issue because of the vast number of clashing property interests. And it had to exercise these powers through a complicated system of courts and bureaus, enforcing them, if necessary, through the aid of armed might."

Eroscheen seemed to have finished and Yonne did not press the matter. Like so many other things, it sounded unacceptably Utopian. Surely, he knew that the age-old tensions upon Earth between sovereign states, which at times flared up into the mass violence we knew as wars, could not be resolved so easily as these Vinibins claimed they had resolved them. Perhaps, in their eagerness to impress him they had overstated things a bit. We on Earth would have done that. Perhaps, the true state of affairs would come out when he travelled about to see for himself.

So he asked what seemed a noncontroversial question: How did Vinibins manage to carry on an orderly exchange of goods and services and even knowledge between nations without some form of political organization broader in outlook than mere production bodies? To his surprise, Eroscheen voiced the very thought he himself had been harboring.

"I have, perhaps, overstated the absence of a political structure, Sir Yonne, because in our discussion we were pre-

185

occupied with the ancient coercive type of state. We do have various forms and levels of broad political organization. They integrate the free association of Vinibins across the planet.

"Oh," said Yonne, still a bit dubious.

"If you will think of us Vinibins as pursuing our educational and productive objectives, or those of any other common venture, from a twofold standpoint—a local and a global one—it will help you to understand our way of life. Every Vinibin enterprise has first its specific, creative purpose; then, its general, coordinative one. The administrative techniques and policies within the first are directed towards a definite local function, whether that be the production of food and clothing or the performance of opera, music, games or scientific research. Allowing the fullest play of Socio autonomy in these things, Vinibins are equally concerned with the coordination of their local creative efforts into well-integrated planetary goals to insure equitable distribution of the total produce.

"It is in this second aspect of Vinibin endeavors, Sir Yonne, that the political functions we almost overlooked apply. They are expressed through a complex network of planning, administrative and coordinating bodies. At the highest policy levels we seek the guidance of the Chieftains at the Eternal Circles, of whose detached judgments we are assured."

Yonne could not help but be impressed by this remarkable analysis from so youthful a Vinibin as Eroscheen. "Do you mean," he asked, "that the political branch in production directs inter-Socio policy and distribution?"

"Exactly—and intercontinental policy too."

"Well," said Yonne, "perhaps you have merely destroyed one kind of state authority for a new one? Perhaps, this gives these . . . ah, political executives the same kind of power over their fellow Vinibins as . . . ?"

"As what?" asked Eroscheen.

Yonne decided to withhold for a while the worldly picture as he knew it. He said, however, with a sly wink: "Could it be that you Vinibins have only transferred the powers of property and the state to a new citadel—to the directors of production?"

Eroscheen observed Yonne thoughtfully. "There never has been such a transference," he said finally. Then he grinned as though he suddenly saw at what Yonne was driving. "No, Sir Yonne, that power has surely disappeared . . . and it will never return. It can't. You must remember the principle of multiple productive service. Every director of productive policy is also a manual worker. That makes a vast difference! It wipes out the arrogance of status as completely as once the introduction of collective production wiped out the arrogance of property. You will soon discover that."

"I shall look forward to it. Tell me, how do these directors come into their high office?"

"Much the same way as candidates for any administrative office. They are elected."

"Elected?"

"Yes."

"Hm—that's cumbersome, isn't it? And it doesn't necessarily get the best man."

"It does. But it must be an intelligent method, Sir Yonne. It cannot be a mere counting of heads, like the counting of sacks of potatoes or cabbage. It must be intelligently democratic."

"Ah yes, Eroscheen . . . now you make me truly curious! How do you make democracy intelligent? That really interests me!"

"You are asking me, Sir Yonne? . . . You, a human being!" Eroscheen eyed Yonne and laughed strangely.

Yonne flushed. It seemed as though they were suddenly parrying swords, this young Vinibin and he. Each time he sought a vulnerable spot in the Vinibin coat of armor, Eroscheen repulsed him with ease. Every offensive thrust, seemed to be turned quickly against him. He was forever on the defensive. Eroscheen had a natural advantage. The terms of the encounter were all his. Yonne was a novice, a total stranger. It was not a fair match!

XII

Their first visit that afternoon was to the "Global Conveyor." Returning to the transportation bureau, they ascended a spiral stairway leading to the "roof" of the artery. They walked. They came out upon an observation platform about twenty feet long enclosed by a solid rail. A single gate led out to the tracks—tracks, unlike any Yonne had ever seen.

The entire right-of-way was about six hundred feet wide, and contained six "tracks." They were really not tracks at all in the sense of rails running parallel along a flat surface, but huge triangular flutes or depressions running side by side along the top of the artery like a series of irrigation channels drained of the water.

The two flutes along the center were the largest, perhaps thirty feet deep and forty feet wide, with the sides sloping downward at an angle of forty-five degrees until they met. The remaining four flutes, two on either side of the central ones, were somewhat smaller. At the bottom of each flute, where the sides converged like a triangle ran a single rail, or what looked like a rail. Near the top of each sloping side also was a rail—making altogether three rails for each flute.

All the rails glistened like mercury, and Yonne learned from Eroscheen that they did, in fact, contain a highly compressed fluid. The contracted surface of this liquid was stronger than the finest steel and almost frictionless. Eroscheen explained the principle of the unusual structure.

"The lower portion of the conveyor coaches," he said, "fits into these triangular flutes like the keel of a ship. The conveyor does not run on wheels, but glides on its keel along the bottom rail on a single runner. Contact with the side rails is slight at any time, usually only when the conveyor is moving slowly or at a standstill. Otherwise, the coaches are free running without rail contact or friction. The side rails are only a secondary lateral support; equilibrium is attained by large gyroscopes placed along the center of gravity of the conveyor to set up lines of force in the forward direction and against side sway."

There was a faint whistling sound that grew increasingly louder. Eroscheen said quickly:

"Hold on to the rail, Sir Yonne. One is coming now."

A small gray spot loomed in the distance and gradually grew larger. In a few seconds Yonne could make out the front view of a conveyor coming along one of the center flutes. The lower half tapered to a point like the hulk of a ship and protruded downward toward the bottom rail. The upper portion was obloid in shape, a little wider than high. At the top he noticed a semicircular projection. Before he had time to make further observation, the conveyor was upon them—and gone!

Altogether noiseless, except for a thin, whistling sound with which it cut the atmosphere, it shot past them at terrific speed. In a few moments it was again out of sight!

189

Yonne had never seen anything quite so fast on land or in air. It made a jet plane look like a hanging blimp.

"Whew!" he cried, "what speed!"

"It makes only a limited number of stops," said Eroscheen. "Ten in all—and it completes the twelve thousand mile journey in less than four hours."

"In what?"

"Four hours."

"Three thousand miles an hour?"

"A little more than that," said Eroscheen simply, "counting the stops. Of course, the local conveyors on the outer tracks do less."

"Really!"

"Yes."

Yonne was still holding on to the platform rail against the powerful suction created by the passing conveyor. "Eroscheen," he exclaimed, "you have been holding out on me!"

Eroscheen didn't catch Yonne's meaning and only replied with the thought uppermost in his mind. "It is a curious thing," he said, "but the means of locomotion is identical to that used by your own airship, Sir Yonne. We employ jet propulsion. Yet, we have never thought of flying! You saw the circular tube extending along the top of the conveyor . . . ?"

Yonne nodded. Yes, he wondered too. If Vinibins had advanced to such a high degree of engineering, why had they never learned how to fly? How could the inventive genius of a whole planetary people express itself so fully along certain paths, yet retain this blind spot along a perfectly obvious and related channel? To this question Eroscheen replied with perplexity.

"That is what we have been asking ourselves ever since you came. Your achievement illustrates the fascinating mystery of progress. We catch it here; it eludes us completely there."

Still, Yonne couldn't quite reconcile this evidence of Vinibin accomplishment and its limitation. Not to think of flying with all the technical means at their command!

Suddenly, he thought, "Was it really a sign of limitation, or something deeper? We humans had learned to fly. We had for centuries cherished that longing. It was always a romantic idea with us . . . to fly like the birds, far into the heavens, away from Earthly things. Yes, the wish to fly was ancient with us; to soar beyond the sordid reality below; to escape from it, for life was not enough as we humans had fashioned it. Life needed buoyance, beauty. It needed wings. In the thraldom of human affairs, beauty had become a thing elusive. Our quest of it demanded wings.

Vinibins had learned many things—many profound things. They had not learned to fly.

*   *   *   *   *

The huge size of the fleeting conveyor bespoke many comforts. From keel to top it stood about sixty feet high and forty feet wide. It was perhaps six hundred feet long, and resembled the graceful lines of a pleasure yacht.

As with our own vehicles of transportation, its streamlined body facilitated maximum propulsive efficiency. Construction utilized the cambering principle of aircraft wings. When in motion, the conveyor gradually lessened contact with the rails. At full speed, it was free from all material support either from the bottom or side rails.

"You have mastered all the essentials of aviation!" declared Yonne.

"Yes," said Eroscheen, "we realize that now."

The mechanic in Yonne was aroused. "When can we ride in one?" he asked excitedly.

191

"Today," said Eroscheen with a smile. "We shall have to go to the Socio of Guenebe some three hundred miles away where Elan-Coli is making the repairs for the plane. I have made reservations on the next local conveyor which will arrive shortly."

"Splendid!" cried Yonne.

"I'm glad you are pleased. Elan-Coli may need your advice in replacing the damaged parts."

A whistling sound announced the approach of another conveyor. It was of lower pitch, and indicated the lesser speed of a local unit. With extraordinary swiftness, however, the conveyor raced along the track on the far side of the artery, then came to a momentary stop and resumed its journey.

"How do passengers get on and off?" asked Yonne.

"Not above the artery," replied Eroscheen. "These platforms are only for observation purposes. Passengers use the slanting sides."

"The slanting sides?"

"Yes, you will see when we board the unit to Guenebe."

They descended the narrow stairway and returned to the transportation building with its many corridors, circular chambers, and tiny compartments for underground conveyors that led to mysterious places. It all fascinated Yonne. He was impatient to see beyond the countless doors behind which a thousand adventures awaited his human eyes.

They proceeded to a waiting room of the artery station. Entering one of the elevators, they were lifted again to the roof of the artery, this time not out upon the tracks, but just beneath them, or more properly, just under their slanting sides. They came into a long, arched hallway formed by the triangular spaces between the fluted depressions. The walls of the hallway were simply the reverse sides of the conveyor roadbed. Leading out upon the right-of-way were numerous exits, the doors to which were closed.

They were in the artery station, a place in many ways not unlike the waiting rooms of a modern railroad station upon Earth—even to the air of expectancy. It was straight-walled and plain-looking, but held a certain quiet dignity. The high, arched ceiling was sound-proofed and lent a soft echo to the sound of Vinibin voices and footsteps.

Interior decoration was in delicate pastel shades. Oddly designed couches and lounging chairs were placed about for the passengers. The very shape of the room, its elongated, tubelike construction, the mystery of the sealed exits, created an eerie atmosphere, an uncanny sense of motion as though the whole thing and its occupants were being catapulted through space like a bullet.

A lone attendant was on duty in this large and busy place. There were no fares, no tickets to be sold and account-ed for, no concessions. Since all costs of the conveyor services were charged against fixed overhead of the Socio and Prov-inces and all operations depended largely on automation, personnel was at a minimum. The attendant was located on an elevated spot overlooking the whole station, surrounded by instruments and mechanical devices from which he per-formed all the station duties—opening and closing doors, recording and announcing conveyor schedules, counting passengers, flashing signals and so forth.

The absence of the usual commercial activity of an Earthly railroad station was the most conspicuous thing about the place, giving to it an air of informal privacy more like that of a country club than a railroad station. But the air of expectancy was there. It permeated everything. It could be seen on the faces of the Vinibins. Everyone was going places; some on pleasure cruises to friends in near and far-off lands;

others, on "business" trips. There were many children with their teachers, wide-eyed, happy looking youngsters making their first educational journeys.

"Vinibins are always traveling," said Eroscheen. "I suppose none of us ever reaches a ripe old age, ready for the new adventures of unlike form after our Vinibin dissolution, without having first explored every corner of this Vinibin habitat—without first having satisfied to the full the glorious Vinibin wanderlust."

"It's thrilling!" exclaimed Yonne.

"Yes, and the first thrill of the experience never quite leaves one when riding in a conveyor," agreed Eroscheen.

At last the signal was flashed for the arrival of their local. Eroscheen and Yonne took their places as the door slowly opened to reveal the huge conveyor slanting towards the opening. They walked up a kind of gangplank, then entered an elegant vestibule of the conveyor. A broad, curved stairway led to the floor above where rows of private compartments for the travelers extended the length of the conveyor. One of them was reserved for "Eroscheen and Guest." It was exquisitely furnished—as inviting as a stateroom in a luxury steamer. But they did not tarry there. Eroscheen knew Yonne was eager to see things, and he motioned for him to follow. They ascended another stairway to the top floor—the "upper deck."

Entering a spacious dining room in the center of this floor, they were greeted by some passengers seated about. They returned the greetings and continued on through an archway that led to a promenade running the length of the conveyor. Eroscheen pointed to lounging chairs that faced an outside, panelled wall of the conveyor.

"Let us sit here for a moment," he said. "This is the observation balcony from which you can get a good view of the countryside."

194

"A good view?" asked Yonne perplexedly as he looked about for windows. "Where is it?"

Eroscheen chuckled. "I'll show you presently."

They settled back in their chairs. Yonne stretched out his legs in anticipation. "Forgive me for being so impatient," he said, "but when do we start?"

Eroscheen stepped over to the panel and pressed a light control. Instantly, the outside landscape came into view turning itself rapidly upon a wide circle.

"We have already started, Sir Yonne." His face beamed. "How do you like it?"

The conveyor was racing along at great speed. Yonne had not even felt it start, or gain momentum.

The swiftly passing scenery was distinguishable only at a distance, disclosing the arrangement of Vinibin community life. Nowhere did Yonne see places of dense metropolitan population or extensive areas of uninhabited land. Cities and towns—those centers of commerce and industry peculiar to the human social scheme—were completely absent.

There was in this Vinibusian panorama a kind of ebb and flow between spaciously laid out Socios, a continuous stream of communities with widely scattered houses and intermittent sections of farm and timber lands. The artery itself served as a kind of chain of industrial activity that flowed through the Socios, binding them together and coordinating their individual and collective affairs.

From this mere glimpse of some externals of Vinibin social life at Krixlrem and here along the artery, Yonne could see that, technologically, Vinibins were decidedly advanced beyond the human stage. Spiritually, he knew they were on an incalculably loftier plane.

From the dining room now came the sound of animated discussion.

"Listen!" said Eroscheen. "They are talking about the

stranger, Man!" He grinned mischievously. "Let's go in and join the conversation. I promise not to give you away, Sir Yonne."

Yonne was immensely curious, and they entered. The Vinibins were seated about a large table, each with a glass of wine before him. Greeting the new arrivals eagerly, they invited them to join. After an exchange of introductions, Yonne's being a fictitious one, he and Eroscheen sat down and ordered some drinks—via the same automatic service used at the restaurant in Krixlrem.

The passengers, knowing the two had just boarded the conveyor at Krixlrem, were avid for news. Did Yonne and Eroscheen know that the stranger, Man, had landed there in his airship? Eroscheen nodded. Did they know he had found the Chieftains safe on the island of Kommschein? Eroscheen nodded again, and there was a twinkle in his eyes. An elderly Vinibin leaned forward:

"It is said the Man is making some repairs on the airship at Krixlrem." Then, in an awesome whisper, "Did you get a chance to see him?"

"We not only saw him," boasted Eroscheen, "we spoke with him!"

"What!"

"We saw his ship."

"You don't say!" There was sensation, and all the party crowded about them.

"What does he look like?"

Eroscheen screwed up his nose. "Oh, not unlike us Vinibins," he said placidly and nudged Yonne for a comment.

"They say he resembles a Namuh," Yonne suggested.

"A Namuh!" exclaimed the guests in horror.

Yonne had learned from Vergia that the Namuh were a queer species of beings inhabiting a remote region of Vinibus. They were a cross between a prehistoric stock of

Vinibins and an order of simians now extinct. They clung to a primitive form of living that was neither apelike nor Vinibin, a kind of twilight existence from which they seemed incapable of emerging.

"A Namuh? No!" Amazement went down the line. Yonne looked at Eroscheen.

"What do you think?" he asked him.

Eroscheen not realizing that Yonne already knew about this unfortunate race, was taken a little aback by the remark, but he kept a serious face.

"There may be a resemblance," he admitted, "but it is a very slight one."

"Strange," declared the others. "And so heroic a Man!"

They all felt quite sorry for Yonne.

The elderly Vinibin was not interested in appearances. In his eyes there was a faraway look.

"Man's airship is a remarkable thing," he said. "Still, it seems to be a rather crude affair, mechanically. The Man had great courage to dare so vast a journey in it." The old Vinibin scrutinized Yonne. "It has remarkable possibilities, this airship, though it moves but clumsily."

"Ah!—there I agree with you!" declared Yonne. "Very clumsily and *slowly* when compared to your splendid conveyors—*our* splendid conveyors," he added hastily. The old Vinibin raised his brows. The members of the party exchanged puzzled looks. The old Vinibin spoke again.

"The Man has done a noble thing. He has brought together the peoples of two planets. A new era awaits the Vinibins of the future."

"A new era awaits Humans and Vinibins alike!" replied Yonne with emotion.

"Yes," said the Vinibin. There was a solemn murmur of assent from the others.

* * * * *

197

They were approaching Guenebe; so they had to take leave of their fellow passengers.

At Guenebe they set out directly for the manufactory, where they found Elan-Coli at work on the repairs. The establishment covered many acres of ground and specialized in the production of conveyor coaches. To Yonne it was a familiar scene: huge cranes and hoists; lathes, shapers, presses, and a great variety of other machine shop equipment; foundries, smelting ovens, and a host of mechanical devices and equipment quite unfamiliar to him.

Again, since it was past noon, production was not in progress. Only Elan-Coli and a select group of technicians and mechanics were present engaged in constructing the new wing. The remarkable thing about these Vinibins was that they went about their tasks with a leisurely tempo, yet they evidenced a speed of accomplishment through mechanical finesse that was astounding. Yonne congratulated Elan-Coli.

"You are making rapid progress."

"You wanted it quickly," he answered with a broad smile.

"Thank you."

Elan-Coli bowed. "It will be ready by noon tomorrow."

"So soon?"

Now Yonne felt disappointed because he wanted time to see the Youth Community. Eroscheen caught the tone in his voice and grinned with pleasure.

"We shall have time to go there, Sir Yonne. The Youth Activities begin early in the morning."

"Fine! I am looking forward to that visit."

* * * *

They left Elan-Coli and his assistants, for there was no need for Yonne's assistance. It was clear that these Vinibins could easily have restored a complete new craft in short order had he presented the task to them. The reason for all this technical ingenuity was presently to be disclosed to him. He was about to see an example of Vinibin educational theory and practice at the Youth Community that would make human efforts look feeble indeed.

XIII

They lodged that night in Guenebe in one of the many attractive country inns maintained all over Vinibus to accommodate the heavy volume of traveling. At dawn they set out for the Youth Community.

Yonne was full of questions, for he was confused on many things. For one thing, his first direct observations here were in two fields in which Vinibins, contrary to impressions he had gained at the Eternal Circle and from Eroscheen's remarks, followed the same centralized, large-scale practices as humans did: Transportation and Communication. He began to think these were typical.

"Indeed, no!" declared Eroscheen vigorously. "We do not have mass production or specialization or centralization. Nothing is further from the truth! Nearly all Vinibin primary productive enterprises are local in character to meet the needs of a single Socio, or at most, as in the case of some semi-public services like lighting and heating, of a small group of adjacent Socios.

"You see, Sir Yonne, while the best productive techniques known to Vinibins are fully available to all Socios, their application is left to each community. You will find much diversity in mechanical detail as you travel about Vinibus; and for this reason you will find each Socio possessing a distinct individuality and character.

"Localism in management and technique upon Vinibus is an essential condition not only for the fullest creative development but also for the most flexible practices. It assures us a free interplay, on the widest possible scope, of new and old ideas. And what is very important, Sir Yonne, it enables us to keep all the individual productive establishments reasonably small and independent in function. The massing of too great an investment in a single set of equipment and machines is thereby prevented. Failure to guard against such concentration would make it prohibitive for us to alter radically old techniques for new and better ones because of the huge social cost involved in the replacement. No, we Vinibins have found it far more economical and interesting to decentralize the administrative and productive mechanism while we centralize only essential controls. Total planetary budgeting and accounting, equitable distribution of all Vinibusian resources, common accessibility to the best productive practices—these are the proper subjects for centralization." Eroscheen paused.

"Do you understand what I mean?"

Yonne understood, and he thought of the vast number of inventions on Earth held unused in the archives of business corporations—corporations that he remembered were gigantic enough, yet too small as individual investors to command the resources needed for prompt replacement of obsolete equipment.

What an anomalous thing this Earthly condition was. Despite all the loose talk of individual initiative, he now saw from his new vantage point upon Vinibus that these corporations were not truly progressive because they were not truly big enough in the concepts of their objectives.

200

Thus, they were more often an obstacle than an asset to progress and well-being, a lag rather than a spur to scientific and technological advancement.

How different it was upon Vinibus! Here, no venture was too small to command the support of the whole population, no project too great to prevent a single Socio from undertaking it. Local autonomy was complete, but it stood on the firm base of social cooperation.

He listened with rapt attention to Eroscheen's description of the broader Vinibin relationships, across the entire planet, consequent upon those Vinibin productive practices.

No notion of state sovereignty was there! That legalized halo of particularism in human affairs had long been discarded upon Vinibus. Long discarded had been that separatism between the peoples of all lands, which seemed with us always to have but one consequence, the enrichment of private plunderers through the dark medium of nationalistic hatreds and wars. There was no place in Vinibin thinking for hatred against a "foreign" enemy, because the idea of kinship transcended far beyond geographic, ethnic, even biological lines. In an all-inclusive sense it brought Vinibins close together as immediate kin in the infinite setting of interspecies relationships.

More clearly than ever before, did Yonne now divine the ugly connotation of that human word, *foreigner,* that loathsome concept more sinister in its power for evil, more ghastly in its ravishment of the very soul of man than all the instruments of the wars it begot.

It was well, thought Yonne now, that he had imbibed something of the fundamental Vinibin ideology at the Cypress Circle. He was grateful to the Chieftains and conscious of their wisdom. They had enabled him to comprehend the genesis of the particulars about him; to understand the whole complex structure of a world society dedicated to the twofold proposition of safeguarding collective security and personal liberty. He had learned from them too, that the absence of private title to property did not mean of necessity its replacement by any paternalistic notions of state ownership. In the Kinship of All Living Things there was simply no place for the concept of ownership, whether by the individual or by the state. Neither the laissez-faireism of private capital nor the bureaucracy of a superstate was a part of Vinibin social philosophy. These wise people, recognizing the inviolability of all forms of life, even of all "inanimate things," could never think in terms of chattel holdings either between Vinibin and Vinibin, or between Vinibins and Things.

Vinibins worshipped a new kind of rugged individualism, an individualism conditioned by a social synthesis, which, thought Yonne, human beings can never hope to emulate.

"Never?" He asked himself. "Never? Why not? These Vinibins are no different biologically from their kin on Earth. They live in similar material environs. They are, in fact, so much like us humans that I continually fuse the two in my comparative judgments!"

Eroscheen interrupted his musings to bring him back to the subject of their visit.

"The Youth Community, Sir Yonne, will give you a preview of our Vinibin adult world. I am impatient to see what you think of it!"

"And I am impatient too," declared Yonne.

They came to the miniature artery surrounding the Youth Community of Guenebe and entered. Two things impressed Yonne at once: the similarity of the place to a university campus, and also its unmistakable contrast to one. Though much larger in area than a university, the grounds contained many of the characteristic college buildings, the student dormitories, the familiar lawns, the benches placed beneath shade trees, the quiet, cloistered air.

And the students too! Some were on their way to classes; others were strolling on the grass or chatting in small groups about the work and plans of the day. The age range was lower than that of college students—somewhere between fourteen and twenty years. One had to look a little closer at the individuals themselves to note another difference: their faces, their posture, their physical condition. These youngsters were strikingly vigorous looking, the boys with erect and stalwart bodies; the girls, like all Vinibin females Yonne had yet seen, exceedingly beautiful, and endowed with an exquisite grace of movement.

The fine bodies of these youths lent an amorous touch to the scene. They made an arresting picture in vivid contrast to the more staid and physically underdeveloped scholastic groups Yonne had known on Earth. The comparison was almost painful and gave him a feeling akin to compassion for his human colleagues.

There was reason for all this. He had to remind himself constantly that this was *not* a college campus, and its members were *not* the products of our human educational system.

As they walked about the grounds they saw many different groups of students, and each group was garbed in its own distinctive costume. Variation in dress was extreme and without apparent coherence. The individuals looked as though they were participating in some kind of theatrical or historical pageant. To Yonne's question, Eroscheen replied:

"This is exactly what the costumes represent—a historical pageant."

"In this place of learning?"

"Yes. It has become traditional in many Youth Communities for the members to adopt the costumes of Vinibins whose historical occupations they are studying. For instance, the younger students, receiving training in the ways of life of an earlier day, wear the costumes of those historical periods. Partly for the pleasure of imitation, partly for color and reality it lends to their tasks, youths take eagerly to this art of dress, and strive to outdo each other in reproducing faithfully the periods they represent. They do this not only in dress and mannerism, but also in occupational techniques. In this respect theirs is still a child-world of make-believe."

The idea struck Yonne as slightly farfetched. Eroscheen went on to elaborate:

"Primary productive education proceeds along the course of historical development. Direct training in a given skill begins with the earliest known methods and leads finally to a mastery of contemporary ones. You will note this, Sir Yonne, when we visit the establishments at the Youth artery. It is an approach that has great value because it instills in the minds of students a sense of growth and fluidity in all services and skills. It heightens comparative judgment, and, doing so, assures a broad understanding of one's place in the total scheme of occupational relationships. Finally, it fosters an inventiveness of mind that is something amazing, even before the adult stage."

Eroscheen smiled reminiscently. "Wearing the dress of our ancestors," he said, "while working in a native setting, with traditional tools and equipments, is great fun. And it is constructive. You live again through the whole gamut of occupational history in an atmosphere of realism."

Yonne observed an attractive-looking couple, a youth and his girl companion, passing close by. They were of the older age group and, strolling arm-in-arm, were deeply engrossed in each other.

204

"Those two are mates," said Eroscheen with a grin.

"How do you mean?"

"Well, they are mates. You know . . ."

"I'm afraid I don't," said Yonne.

"Well, they live together—cohabit as male and female. They . . ." He looked at Yonne still grinning. "They are in love, just as you, Sir Yonne."

"I don't understand. They live together?"

"Yes."

"They're married?"

"Huh?"

"Skip it!" said Yonne remembering their last entanglement on the subject.

Indicating a remote wooded section of the grounds where stood some quaint houses hidden among the trees, Eroscheen said:

"You see those love nests over there?"

"Yes."

"They are for the romantic young couples."

"For what?"

"The romantic couples."

Yonne bristled with human indignation. "What is this, an institution of learning or a . . . free love colony?"

"Free love?" Eroscheen stared at him, then burst into laughter. "Do human beings on Earth, perchance, set a price on love?" he asked mirthfully. "We Vinibins don't even apply that charge to fixed overhead—except, of course, for the cost of the progeny!"

"You are joking, Eroscheen."

"I, Sir Yonne?"

"You don't mean to tell me that these young folks scarcely out of their teens, and still in their years of training, are free to . . . to . . . well, to indulge in promiscuous sex relations."

"But, Sir Yonne!" came back Eroscheen with his own display of Vinibin indignation, "not promiscuous relations! We shouldn't approve of that!"

"You shouldn't approve of it?"

". . . We frown upon it."

"You frown upon it! . . . Is that all?"

Eroscheen nodded dubiously.

Yonne was becoming exasperated with him. "Come, you will have to stop speaking in riddles."

"Are you serious, Sir Yonne?"

"Am I serious! Didn't you just intimate that you have a kind of free love colony here? Well, you really can't expect me to understand all this. I am a stranger from Earth, you know."

"Of course, of course," said Eroscheen apologetically. "I am always forgetting."

His enigmatical manner left Yonne uncertain whether to remain angry or not. "Please get to the point," he said a bit impatiently.

"I'll try to explain it to you, Sir Yonne." Eroscheen cogitated, then said:

"It is a long story, and the custom is a very old one. Going back to the earliest days of Dilphon-Mosa, we find that members of Youth Communities begin to mate during the last years of their residence. Naturally," he added in a voice that took it for an elementary fact, "one begins to feel an infatuation for the opposite sex as bodily maturity occurs. The physical side of love demands release." He paused, wondering why he was going to the trouble of explaining such obvious things to Yonne, his hero from Earth.

Yonne, sensible human that he was, found himself nodding approval. "All right, go on."

"It has come to be the accepted thing, Sir Yonne, that

sexual mating takes place in Youth Communities during the last year. Of course, there is really no need for any encouragement." He laughed. "The desire comes quite of its own volition! And at a logical time, too. One begins for the first time to grow conscious of the creative potentialities of the self. One begins to look forward eagerly to entering the adult world with its genuine productive responsibilities. In this romantic setting incipient love finds its natural place. And so you will find it a common occurrence at a Youth Community for young couples in the first throes of sexual love, to be escorted to their nuptial domicile by fellow students, in frolicsome ceremony and serenading."

"Hm . . ." Yonne found himself saying, ". . . may be right enough biologically, but . . . Gosh!" All the age-old moral precepts in the human code descended upon him. He struggled valiantly with them then said almost timidly, "You say it's a common occurrence?"

"Common enough, Sir Yonne, though not true for everyone, of course. We don't all mature alike or at the same time. And in this as in all things, restraint until the proper time is taught our youth."

"And the union—how long does it last?"

"For a life-time, maybe; for a shorter period, perhaps; for not even the duration of the year, usually."

"Hm . . . As I thought! . . . and the children?"

"The children?" It was Eroscheen's turn to be shocked. "Not in the first year, Sir Yonne!"

"I see . . . A sort of trial affair!"

"Yes—but we seldom attach even that much motive to it. Call it just the first thrill of mating—the awakening of sexual love."

"Oh—then this is only a kind of partial love?" The cynicism in Yonne's tone was unconcealed, but Eroscheen missed it. He shook his head vigorously.

"Indeed, no, Sir Yonne! First love is no partial love—not if I know anything about it! First love is full . . . full to overflowing. It is passionate, unstinting." He knit his brow in a valiant effort to probe the Earthly visitor's lack of understanding. "Perhaps you mean, Sir Yonne, that first love is a young love . . . a transitory love?"

Yonne was no longer sure what he meant. He blurted out his next question.

"Then, there are other matings to follow?"

"Other matings? Oh, certainly . . . in most cases. Sooner or later, however, one finds himself, either to mate for life, or, well, to journey alone, loving with reservations as it were; sharing the companionship of the one you love occasionally as mutual desire may dictate."

"Mutual desire? Huh! . . . And what becomes of all the broken hearts?"

"The broken hearts?"

"Yes, the anguish caused by the craving for a more constant love than the errant mate might offer."

"I don't understand you, Sir Yonne."

"Very well, then what becomes of the mate who does not want to terminate the union when the other does?"

Eroscheen was mystified.

"If you mean that one may love more intensely, more enduringly than the other, then there is, of course, an ill-balanced mating. Those things happen upon Vinibus, to be sure. There are some aching hearts—though we should hardly call them broken ones." He studied Yonne, unable to see just why he could not comprehend. With an almost pleading voice he went on: "Don't you see, Sir Yonne, this is why Vinibins love early in life, that they may learn to love well. Youth matings upon Vinibins are but superficial, mere sexual groping, as transitory usually, as they are passionate. It takes a long time and much experience to

208

find deep and lasting love. In this respect, are we not like human beings, Sir Yonne?"

Like human beings? Yonne's brain was in a whirl. He didn't know. He thought of Vergia. Had she loved before—like this? She was beautiful—and desirable! And she was older than these youths! With a human pang, he realized: Their love would not be the first! There were others . . . other matings . . . many others! The thought was maddening . . . Then, strangely, he felt something recoil within him. He seemed to be struggling against himself, the human being versus the newborn Vinibin! In his thoughts there loomed suddenly a horrible idea. Like an emblazoned meteor it flashed across his vision, and it hurled itself against his brain, and it thundered out its accusation: *"PROPERTY!"*

Eroscheen's voice came cheerfully to break into his crazy train of thoughts.

"Sir Yonne, we have arrived at the Youth Community's class in shoemaking. Shall we go in?"

"Shoemaking?" mumbled Yonne incoherently. "Why, yes, let us enter."

Classes had begun. It was a beginning unit, and the students were all boys between twelve and fourteen years of age. The place was busy as a beehive. The whole department in shoemaking, he noticed, from classes in the earliest to the latest methods, extended a considerable length along the artery. It resembled an industrial exhibit—except that its purpose was not to educate the public, but the student. It might easily have been mistaken by Yonne for a kind of Vinibin industrial school, but such an observation would have been a distorted one.

Visitors were frequent at the Youth Community; so they were free to move about without questioning. The boys in early methods were engaged in the simple craft of the ancient cobbler. Seated on crude wooden chairs made by fellow students in elementary furniture construction, they worked diligently at their tasks; curing, hammering, cutting, perforating, and shaping the shoes with awl and knife, and sewing together the finished product by hand. They were dressed in the scanty garment of an earlier day, consisting of knee breeches; a plain, open blouse; leather apron, and shoes of the student's own manufacture. The shoes were of simple design, but sturdy. Each pupil proudly turned out a goodly number of them to meet the requirements of other youngsters of his own age.

This was typical. Students in this ancient craft as in others, produced for use as well as for their own education. And, before a youth grew to adult status he had progressed in many subjects in his vocational training. If he took a fancy to a given craft, and his recorded skill warranted it, he adopted it as one of his primary adult services. He learned many skills—in fact, he began with a complete survey of all of them during the first years, and only gradually narrowed the field to those of a likely choice.

They went from shoemaking classes to one in heavy industry. Students here were engaged in extracting an industrial "metal" from its crude raw state. The raw material was not mined in the traditional manner, but was derived from products grown and cultivated much as we raise soy bean or the rubber plant. Stalwart youngsters—there were again no girls in the class—were skillfully manipulating mechanical devices for purifying the raw materials, separating them into their elements, combining them again according to Vinibin formulae, putting them through treatment processes from which came eventually the finished product. Yonne took this to be an example of modern technique, but Eroscheen informed him that it was quite an antiquated one.

They made the rounds of other shops and classes along the artery. They could not visit all, but Yonne could see the classes covered virtually all branches of primary production, and that each branch was broken down into units dealing with essential developmental stages. Sample products were displayed in show windows and exhibition rooms. The bulk was for direct use in the Socio, but some surplus produce was stored or shipped to other provinces lacking in raw materials or possessing unfavorable conditions for their use in education. For shipping purposes, the Youth Community artery made underground connections with the regular transportation system.

Though the Youth Community was co-educational, the sexes specialized in skills applicable for the most part to their own needs. Boys generally studied production in those services and goods required by the male sex. Girls, true to the feminine ideal even as on Earth, participated in the domestic arts, in primary production for infant needs and training, and in the physically lighter assignments. From this it must not be assumed, however, that their education was not co-ordinate with or less inclusive than that of boys; there was merely a difference of emphasis on particulars.

From the technical side, Yonne knew there was nothing remarkable about all this. While he knew too that we have any number of schools for trade and occupational training on Earth, he realized that what he saw here was something vastly different. When he remembered that this training on the purely mechanical and physical side of production was extended to every single youth attaining the age of twelve or fourteen, that it was only a first part of the education of *all members of society,* the program of the Youth Community assumed a new and astounding significance. Performance and service, these were the first things in Vinibin education. Historical cultures, ethics, literature, philosophy, technology—these were the last things reserved for the adult education period.

But youth education in primary production was only half the curriculum. To it was added the equally important part played by Aesthetics, which called for instruction in the fields of art, music, painting, gymnastics, recreation, and so forth. It was carried on during the afternoon hours. Emphasis in the beginning again centered on performance, not on history or genetics or appreciation, though these played an increasingly important role in the advanced stages of education.

They had no opportunity to visit classes in aesthetics since these were not in session. But their work was becoming perfectly clear to Yonne. There young Vinibins were taught to develop the artistic, the creative, the beauty and pleasure-seeking side of their nature and their productive service. Important above all: These youngsters were the same ones who participated in the morning's production classes.

In aesthetic educational production also they exhibited their works to the adult population in neighboring Socios. Many of the samples of art and handicraft were eagerly purchased by visitors and tourists.

Vinibin youth observed an interesting practice in this respect. Each productive or aesthetic service commanded its purchase price as judged by "previews" conducted by fellow students and faculty. Students vied with each other to excel in the originality, the beauty or utility of their accomplishments. Receipts from the public, i.e., the visiting adult population, were credited to the student's "Youth Community Account." This account recorded the costs of his education against the value of everything he produced, beginning on the day he entered the Youth Community.

Often the artistic creation of some gifted pupil would

command an exceptionally high price. That would greatly boost the credit side of his account!

Unlike aesthetic educational production, primary production classes were collective in nature, with emphasis on collective education, not on individuality of the product. They could not serve, therefore, to vary the status of the student's account very much. The variable rested with his aesthetic contributions. There developed as a result a keen and an exciting competitive struggle. The quest for honors in aesthetic accomplishment gave zest to the student's labors which doubly enriched him and the community. Proud was the boy who left the Youth Community to enter adult society with an enviable credit side to his Youth Account!

The young Vinibin's graduation from the Youth Community disclosed to Yonne another interesting practice. The transition to full-fledged adult status called for a complicated and far-reaching piece of social engineering such as the human race had hardly begun to dream of. With the educational data complete, and the Youth's multiple vocational qualifications established, induction into the adult services became a matter of the greatest social and individual importance. The transfer had to proceed with a view towards meeting the varying and complex personnel needs of adult production. To educate a youth without assurance of his satisfactory promotion into the economic structure in accordance with his multiple vocational qualifications, would have been rank folly in the eyes of Vinibins. Thus, it may be readily seen that the educational program in every Socio throughout Vinibus had to be integrated with the total social situation, varying from year to year in its occupational and aesthetic emphasis, as the dictates of global economy demanded.

Yonne learned that this did not mean regimentation,

but an orderly transfer of young Vinibins from the centers of education to those of production. Above all, it guaranteed to the individual a fruitful termination of his training period to be followed by one of social usefulness.

* * * * *

Returning to their room after the visit, they talked late into the night on the implications of what Yonne had seen.

The inevitable operation of justice in this educational process began to unfold itself to him. Yonne recalled the familiar phrase used on Earth whenever it was necessary to apologize for a particularly discouraging bit of human behavior: "That's human nature, and you can't change it!"

Vinibin nature had undergone many changes since the days of Dilphon-Mosa. In one respect alone, as a result of the integration of educational and productive services, it had been changed profoundly. Yonne had already witnessed it in the few Vinibins he had met. There was in the Vinibin personality a blending of modesty and self-assurance that mirrored the fine adjustment of the individual to his social environment.

Careerism upon Vinibus was unknown. Success in one's chosen proficiencies was dependent not upon any irrelevant technique of cunning and connivance, of self-assertiveness and flattery, of unprincipled opportunism or genteel bribery. This human technique was expressive only of the oddities of the human situation. Upon Vinibus success in its external quality was a matter of demonstrated qualification and performance, pure and simple. In its deeper, inner sense, it was the balanced unfolding of the psycho-physical organism; so that the individual might live in complete harmony, not only with his fellow Vinibins, but with himself.

Yonne soon learned that "careerism"—and the term applied not just to the successful upon Earth who had "arrived," but as well to the hordes of humankind, all aspiring to achieve "success"—careerism was a phenomenon peculiar to the human scene. But human though it was, it was not a thing immutable or original. Plainly, Yonne could see now that it was the individual's protective reaction to an environment of common insecurity; for no human being was safe from the specter of poverty and want, if he failed. Education was no guarantee. Human education failed doubly of its function. On the one hand, it burdened the individual with an irrational, upside-down cultural equipment; on the other, it washed its hands of him when it turned him out into the adult world. Protection against want in the adult world lay in one direction only: in the acceptance of, and the adaptation to the laws of the jungle. Thus did the struggle for personal success upon Earth become inextricably associated with the cunning of the fox, and with the habit of the vulture feeding upon the carcasses of the fallen dead.

In his brief and thought-provoking experience at the Youth Community of Guenebe, Yonne suddenly beheld the human scene with shocking clarity. He could see in bold relief the social setting that accounted for the "human nature" of his day. He saw through the absurdity of the notion that the individual gives to society the tone and color that makes it good or bad as he is good or bad. He saw that society is not a mere aggregate of individuals, but that it exists as an organic whole at the individual's birth. It nurses and moulds and eventually crystallizes his character into the acquired shape we call human nature. Of this there was no longer any doubt—nor of the fact that the individual plays a reciprocal role in his social and hereditary environment; else, there should never have been a Krixlrem, a Guenebe, a Dilphon-Mosa! In his singular position against a background of historical and contemporary mores, the individual gave something precious of his unique individuality; but he received infinitely more than he gave (for as a single individual he was less than the collective whole) and what he gave had been distilled through the all-pervasive social medium of which his contribution was but a part.

*　　*　　*　　*　　*

To Yonne's human mind the visit to the Youth Community of Guenebe was the final stimulus that completed his spiritual transformation. Up to then he had been confused and baffled, torn between opposing concepts—the Human and the Vinibin—unable fully to rid himself of the former or to adapt himself to the latter. On this occasion, however, as he traversed the grounds of this remarkable Vinibin university, a university in the literal sense, where instruction in the arts and crafts was truly inclusive of all vital things, and for every Vinibin—a university of all the people—he found himself at last.

As a result he longed to bring to an end his inactive role, happy in the thought that he was still young and of receptive mind for the new Vinibin experiences. He wanted to meet Vinibins, to know them intimately. He wanted to become one of them, feeling sure that there must be a place for him in their social scheme. His original ardour for bringing human enlightenment to the planet had long subsided. As once he had abandoned all hope of ever being able to return to Earth, so now he lost all desire of ever doing so.

On that eventful morning at Guenebe the human being died within Yonne. From this time hence, he was and felt himself a Vinibin!

*　　*　　*　　*　　*

They stood again in the station of the globular artery at Guenebe awaiting the local that would take them back to

Krixlrem. This time, however, Eroscheen and he were not unnoticed. The news of Yonne's identity had leaked out, and at once Vinibins from far and near flocked to see him. Their journey to Krixlrem was turned into a triumphal march with thousands of inspired Vinibins cheering them on the way. Everywhere they were met by vast throngs eager to get a glimpse of the stranger, Man, the greatest mortal since Dilphon-Mosa! How Yonne winced under the encomiums! Yet with it all, he felt he had, unwittingly, but truly widened the spiritual horizon of a whole planetary people.

Amidst tumultuous acclaim they were escorted to the plane by the residents of Krixlrem. Elan-Coli and his associates were awaiting them. With the cheers of the assembled Vinibins ringing in their ears, they ascended again into the wind to resume their journey back to Quiloth.

XIV

Moments of indescribable bliss! Moments that were destined to be short-lived . . . Glorious moments, dwelt in realms of sweetest pleasure!

*   *   *   *   *

It was a mild, tropical evening. The air was clear and all things were bathed in the twilight beauty of the stars. A slight breeze blew from the sea. The moonless sky seemed deeper and more densely black than any Yonne had ever seen on Earth. The stars shone a thousand times more brilliantly and their luster varied markedly to heighten the depth and magnitude of sidereal space. A few silvery gray clouds moved ghostlike across the vaulted Vinibusian heavens, giving a touch of stately motion to the land the stars and the water.

They walked along the shore, Vergia and Yonne, her graceful body leaning lightly upon his arm, her hand clasped in his. They spoke but little, for their hearts were full.

They came to the place on the beach where they had first met. Instinctively they turned to each other, their eyes meeting in tender gratitude for that fateful day.

A silken strand of Vergia's hair brushed against his face. Her glowing gown shimmered in the starlight, and fell close about her shapely body. Yonne stood before her, his eyes drinking in her loveliness. Softly he murmured his love.

She flushed. Her head tilted slightly back, her lips parted to disclose the faintest portion of her pearly teeth.

As they stood there on the shore, the ocean breeze cooling their cheeks, he drew her yielding body to his. She clung to him whispering softly.

"Yonne, dearest, I am happy . . . so happy!"

They strolled along the enchanted beach. Before them, silhouetted dreamily in the pale night, lay the airship.

"Oh, my beloved Vergia!' he sighed. "We shall fly together now!"

"Yes, we shall fly, Yonne—all Vinibins shall fly!"

She held his hand more tightly and nestled closer. "We shall traverse the heavens, Yonne—far out, to the very ends of space!" Between his tender kisses she revealed her dreams: "We shall fly to other planets, and visit your homeland."

"Oho! That I doubt very much."

"Yes, we shall, Yonne dear . . . And we shall visit the people of other planets, too."

Her naïveté was delightful.

218

"But I am serious," she protested. She raised her arm and pointed to the brightest star in all the heavens.

"The planet 'Earth'!" she said fervently. "Your homeland."

Yonne gazed upon it, and his heart filled with a strange yearning.

"My homeland!" He drew her closer.

A wistful look came into her face. "You will return there?"

He reflected, and shook his head.

"You must, Yonne. Your work would not be complete."

"I shall never return."

"Oh!" There was disappointment in her voice.

"You want me to?"

"Yes."

"To leave you?"

"I should go with you, of course."

He smiled.

"Yes . . . We shall go together."

There was more determination in her voice than he could understand.

"Vergia, darling, I would never expose you to so perilous a venture. I made that journey once!"

"I should not be afraid."

She looked trustingly into his eyes, and laid her cheek against his, and they spoke no more of it.

*   *   *   *   *

They came to the plane and entered, for it had now become their trysting place. The evening light came softly through the windows to fall in pale streamers upon the floor. They sat upon the small couch before the cabin window. The luster of the stars was reflected in her gaze as he held her close.

"Vergia . . . darling, at last we have each other!"

"Yes, my dearest . . . !"

Rapturously they kissed, again and again, consumed with the ecstasy of their love. Through the delicate fabric of her gown he gazed upon her lovely body. Caressingly, her hands went to the lapels of his coat, and he drew her passionately to him, kissing her lips, her eyes, her hair . . . Her arms came lovingly about his shoulders . . . And in that wondrous moment they remained clasped in each others arms, silent, trembling, upon the threshold of their union.

* * * * *

Radiant shafts of dawn pierced the eastern sky. The flickering stars struggled vainly to survive, then surrendered, one by one, to the brilliance of the morning sun. Slowly the cabin of the plane became illuminated with the soft glow of morning. They saw the Earthly star, more radiant than all the rest. Boldly it sailed toward the crimson light. They watched it silently. It continued to shine after all the others had long been dimmed.

"Your Homeland!" murmured Vergia as she nestled close to him. "How often have we Vinibins marveled at its bold defiance of the sun."

XV

Long ago, Vergia had sensed the mysterious adumbration of truth. What seemed unthinkable to Yonne in those first delightful hours of their union, she foresaw, even then, as the inevitable sequence of events.

Not many days had passed. He had traveled over the

length and breadth of Vinibus. He had seen what the Chieftains had promised he would see.

Vinibus!—a blessed land, an enchanted island in the vast sea of cosmic space! The longer he stayed upon the planet, the more deeply he became attached to the Vinibin way of life. His former Earthly existence seemed like a shadow of some ignominious past, whence his very soul had miraculously escaped.

Completely and wisely had these Vinibins built, and in building had they learned the subtle art of living well. No vale of tears was theirs. Proudly they might have boasted to Yonne of material progress, but they boasted not. He had seen their manufactories and their institutions of learning—and they far surpassed what humans had built on Earth.

Yet, as he learned to adjust himself to the new world, and to love it dearly, a disconcerting restlessness took hold of him; an unrelenting determination to fulfill the purpose of a strange journey. Vergia's words plagued him:

"You must return to Earth, Yonne. Your work would not be complete."

The Earthly shadow hovered always in the background, refusing to be denied, a stark reality with which he had to reckon. It began increasingly to intrude itself upon his thoughts, until each day became a struggle between desire and inner compulsion. Inevitably, he knew, the conflict must resolve itself in one decision or the other. The more he longed to blot away his Earthly past, to throw himself into this pleasant whirl of Vinibin life, the more insistent grew the deeper urge of conscience.

His work on Vinibus? Absurd! What was there here for him to do? His aeronautical contribution? That had been made, and he knew Vinibins would quickly utilize it for the common good.

His contribution! Once, in jest, he had voiced it to

Bornabi, and he had spoken well: an isolated example of disjointed human achievement.

And there were Bornabi's comments on the early history of Vinibinkind. Antiquity! That is where we humans stood; a thousand years behind these Vinibins, or more! What need had they of him, of those grand services he was once inclined to offer them? The vital question was quite in reverse: What need had human beings of Vinibin aid and guidance?

Vinibins had shown the way! Their course had led from darkness into light. What they had done, humans also could achieve.

Yonne was increasingly steeped in despondent moods. Vergia approached him one day. With tenderness she said:

"Yonne, dearest, I know the specter that is haunting you. I know it, for our love has made us one. The shadow of this specter will darken our lives. It will overwhelm us both to destroy the happiness we have found unless we possess the courage to surmount it."

In her deep brown eyes there was a troubled look. "We must face it, Yonne, and prepare for the perilous journey that will take us to your people. Such is the wondrous call of the Kinship of All Living Things. We cannot fail this call of our nearest kin on Earth."

Her words were spoken gently but they held a fearless determination that he knew was the truth. To try to resist it would be like gorging one's belly with rich food while a beggar pleads for bread.

* * * * *

And so the decision was made. All Vinibus was astir with knowledge of their plan. Once it became known how things really stood upon Earth, there was great approbation of their undertaking. Despite the complete reversal of Yonne's status from one who came to give to one whose people sorely needed Vinibin help, Yonne continued to receive the deepest homage. To Vinibins his coming and leaving confirmed their abiding faith in the infinite unity of all things, and they rejoiced that it should be their lot to contribute to the spiritual progress of their kin upon another planet.

Yonne's own spirit was aflame. Yet there were moments of misgivings. He feared for the human reception of Vinibin ideals—the wondrous truth of the Kinship of All Living Things, that great idea that dwarfed man-made theologies to a level of schoolboy rules and regulations for the attainment of divinity; the fruitful role of Education with its complete reversal of the human order of learning and its orientation toward multiple vocational service for everyone.

The momentous day arrived! All normal activity upon Vinibus was suspended as vast throngs of awe-stricken Vinibins came to witness the take-off on the shores of Quiloth province. A thousand monster ships and yachts, and small boats lay at anchor, dotting the blue surface of the ocean as far as the eye could see. It was a planetary holiday set aside for rejoicing in all lands. Famous choruses, bands and orchestras journeyed to Quiloth to take part in the farewell ceremonies.

Imagination was aroused to undreamed heights. Vinibins hailed the event as the beginning of a new era in the relationship of planetary civilizations. Yonne and Vergia were eulogized as pioneers about to inaugurate an age of interplanetary communication and friendship! They were embarking upon the greatest of all known undertakings—to bring together the peoples of the Universe. They would bring to human beings the glorious story of the Vinibin way of life. Such was the magnificent vision of the Vinibin populace.

The hour arrived! The beach was cleared for the take-off.

Only the Chieftains, Eroscheen and Elan-Coli stood by. Kooklwucs was there too. It sensed something in the atmosphere, for now and then it would nestle close to Vergia, burying its head affectionately in the folds of her dress. When the motors began to roar it became frightened and scampered away venting its displeasure with loud brays, and wiggling its ungainly legs as it jumped nervously up and down. Vergia called it, and, putting her arms about its neck, hugged it silently until it was quiet.

The Quiloth orchestra struck up the now famous anthem dedicated to "The Stranger, Man" and all the choruses joined:

> "Oh, Kinship of All Living Things,
> In this thy consummation lies,
> That from sidereal vistas springs
> A harbinger of Heaven's ties!"

* * * *

The motors spun with a mounting pitch. Gently, the plane taxied over the yellow sand, sailed into the wind . . . over the beautiful land . . . above the glistening sea . . . One last fond glimpse of the Vinibin multitude, of the estate of Bornabi, of the Vinibusian woods and fields, of the stately Cypress Circle, then they turned the nose of the ship out over the ocean . . . up into the vast Heavens.